This book is dedicated to the memory of my dear husband <u>Aleyn R. Jordan</u> and to the memory of <u>Sam</u> for the colouring of <u>Matt</u> and <u>Tigger</u> for many of the escapades herein, with thanks for all their love.

Acknowledgment and many thanks to <u>Robert M. Livie</u> for kindly vetting this book for me, if he will pardon the pun!

Copyright © 2011

Published by Little Cherub Publications, "Huggles"
Great Yarmouth, Norfolk NR30 4LG
Telephone (01493) 856329

First Edition

Printed in Great Brita
R.P.D. Litho Printers, Gorleston-c

GW00630588

Cover design by Valerie

Caricature of Matt the Cat! By Caro Laiey

"Matt the Cat" and illustration ™

ISBN   978-0-9516791-5-9

1

Sunday 11th May

To-day was horrendous – everything had gone, all the rooms were empty, what on earth was going on?

I had woken as soon as the sunlight filtered through the curtains and having lifted my eyelids and given my usual wide yawn as I gradually woke up from my night's slumbers, I'd asked myself, "Do I have to get up?" Yet knowing full well that I would have to, if I wanted to be fed, I'd stretched out my right front leg, followed by my left, then arched my lithe body, I stretched each of my rear legs before somewhat reluctantly stepping out of my warm, soft, fleecy cosy bed.

I had duly padded downstairs to the kitchen – "Good, they had filled my food bowls with juicy chunks of meat, crunchies (good for the teeth, as well as being nutritious) and the essential water bowl. It was only after I had eaten sufficient, that I realised the room was bereft of furniture. No table, chairs, not even my downstairs sofa bed (yep, I was a rich cat – or at least my owners were!). It was also then that I realised that the door to the kitchen had been left open – strange they always shut it at night, in case of fire (they were careful house owners too!).

Next I had noticed that all the normal utensils were missing, the kettle, toaster, microwave, even the kitchen television was gone!

I started to panic now – this was odd.

I ran back into the hall – no umbrella stand, outdoor shoes, even the coat rack was empty.

Normally I am not a nervous cat, in fact I had always considered myself to be independent and not easily rattled, but now I felt another wave of panic sweep over me for as I ran from room to room – they were all empty too. A horrible fear entered my thoughts. Dismissing it, I ran upstairs, perhaps they had cleared downstairs ready for decorating. Despite the still rising panic – I had to stay positive.

I ran along the landing, again noticing all the doors were open, the four bedrooms were all devoid of furniture, even the bathroom had been cleared of towels and toiletries, worse the laundry basket had gone too.

I told myself, yet again, not to panic – there had to be a simple explanation.

Half an hour later I was back in the kitchen, having explored every room in the house. I had leapt up onto every windowsill and peered over the stunning garden at the rear and at the traffic passing along the main road at the front.

I was thirsty now as well as upset. I drank more of my water – strange how it was that most people thought that all cats drank milk – it wasn't true – they mostly drank water. I ate some more food (for thought!). I reminded myself that keeping a sense of humour was essential.

This was getting me nowhere – I had to do something, but what?

All the windows were shut and locked, both front and rear doors were locked - I had tried them. The doors had no cat flaps, so I couldn't even escape outside to explore.

It was then that I heard a noise at the front door – I was at the door in a flash – no one – just the mail falling onto the mat. I even heard the postman beginning to cycle away.

Leaping onto the windowsill nearest the door, I raised my paw and tapped hard on the window. The postman didn't even hear, let alone look back, he was intent on safely negotiating the morning's traffic.

My brain was energized from the rising fear within my little heart as I began to consider my predicament. I reasoned that John and Wanda had not gone on holiday as all the furniture had been removed and I was not being looked after by our kindly neighbours, nor was I in a cattery. Eventually, exhausted, I returned to the comfort of my bed. A nap should refresh me.

The sound of the telephone ringing woke me, suddenly a voice spoke, my spirits lifted and then sank, as I realised it was only the answer phone cutting in. I hoped whoever was ringing might give me a clue as to what was going on, but no, whoever had telephoned was one of those people who hated answer phones, so not even a message was left. I suddenly yawned and settled down again, I really didn't want to think any more – I just wanted to sleep away the rest of the day.

Monday 12th May

The early May sunlight woke me again this morning and it was beginning to give off some warmth, which was just as well, as I had also realised the heating was off. The sleep had done me some good and I felt my brain was functioning better, at least I thought it was – I was certainly not going to panic like I had done yesterday. I reasoned, that the furniture hadn't been removed ready for the rooms to be decorated and also no one had delivered any newspapers the previous day, so whatever was going on was serious as John and Wanda never missed a day without their newspapers.

I again went through my usual stretching exercises, before padding off to eat some more of my food – luckily I had had the commonsense, even though I was only two years old, that having realised I was truly on my own, I must ration the remaining food and water. So after forcing myself to still leave some food for later, I set off to explore fully my circumstances and if possible find some clues. It was at this time that I noticed that all the curtains and light fittings had been left – "Why?" I asked myself, considering that all the furniture had gone.

Having once more explored the house and still finding no way out of my predicament I once again started to become anxious. The day passed slowly with so little to do, no outside exploring, no chatting with my mates – now I was not only more anxious, but I had to admit, scared. Stupidly, without thinking this time, I had polished off the remainder of the food in the bowl, the only benefit of doing this, was that I managed not to drink all the water.

"Matt, you are a twit," I scolded myself.

The night finally came – at least I didn't mind the dark, but I hated the emptiness and the loneliness of the house now – I missed the sound of voices, people coming and going, nobody to rub myself against, no one to show affection to or receive affection from. I prowled once more around the ground floor of the house, but no, nothing had changed, so climbing the stairs to the landing I perched myself on the windowsill of one of the front bedrooms looking out at the road beyond the drive.

Cars flew past regularly, but none turned into the driveway. I found my

vigil awful and am ashamed to admit a tear fell down my cheek. Eventually, having returned to my bed, I fell asleep and escaped from all my fears.

Tuesday 13th May

What a day! First I was suddenly woken from my slumbers, by a youthful voice shouting "Hey dad, there's a cat up here" – whereupon a strange man, who I later found out was called Jack, had run up the stairs and scooped me up in his arms. His son, whose name turned out to be Shaun, then said, "Gosh dad, he is really handsome. His colouring is unusual – I love the mixture of ginger, black, brown and white."

His dad then said "You can't keep him, you know your mother doesn't like cats."

"But dad….."

"No buts, we will have to find out who he belongs to."

Belongs to, why didn't they ask me I thought. But then they didn't know I had understood every word they had said. Jack continued to hold me in a firm grip and for a while I was glad of the warmth of a human being holding me again. Then, would you believe it, a woman's voice called out.

"Jack, there's a cat's feeding and water bowl in the kitchen as well as a litter tray, can you come and remove them at once please!" Mary, Jack's wife had called up the stairs.

"Coming dear" he had replied.

Jack then had handed me over to Shaun and told him to stay where he was and hurried down the stairs."

I hadn't liked the tone of his wife's voice and thought there was going to be trouble, but I decided to wait and see what transpired first between them. Then came the stream of orders, "Remove these items at once, yes, all of them." Dump them outside, they have no right to be in our home."

Your home I thought – this is my home, not yours – I had begun to think it was about time that I said something. Next, would you believe, Jack had obediently said "Don't worry Mary, I'll take them outside and put them in the black wheelie bin, the previous owners must have one."

"If you find anything else Jack, I want that immediately dumped too," had come the next order.

"What!" I thought, "Had these people no respect for my property." Please don't find my bedding," was my next thought, as I had realised that Mary was one of those women whose dislike of cats was so strong that she couldn't even bring herself to touch anything connected with them and Jack, was a typical wimp of a husband in that he dutifully did everything that was asked of him regardless of what he might have wanted. I even began to feel sorry for him.

I however, needed help immediately

"Shaun, do you think we can creep downstairs and see exactly what is going on please".

That had made Shaun's eyes nearly pop out of his head! "You can talk!" he said.

"And why not, you talk, " I had replied.

This had made Shaun laugh. Good, we are going to get on fine, he had a sense of humour and that's what gets you through life – I was being philosophical now.

Shaun was great, he held me firmly in his arms and crept down the stairs.

We noticed that Jack was taking out a large cardboard storage box that had already been unpacked. It seemed that Mary never did waste time.

"What's your name?" Shaun suddenly asked.

"Matt" I had replied. "Hey, that's cool – you're Matt the Cat!" We had reached the bottom of the stairs now and Shaun crept across the hall towards the kitchen door. We both noticed that Mary was busy unpacking yet more boxes marked kitchen.

Jack re-entered and hovered, awaiting his next orders.

"Mum's a bit of a control freak, you know Matt, but she has some good points – she is very efficient, she will have this lot unpacked and sorted soon; you see the kitchen is the hub of a home. Dad's a bit scatty and goes off at a tangent if she doesn't control him!" Shaun had continued.

"Jack can you go upstairs and see if there is anything else around relating to a cat" came the next command.

I had panicked at that – there goes my bedding. "Shaun you have to come up with a reason for leaving the house – take me to the neighbours please – they are a lovely genuine couple who have often looked after me, when my owners have gone on holidays."

"Right Matt, don't worry," came his reassuring reply.

"Just popping next door to see the new neighbours mum, I think it's a good idea to meet them as soon as possible, don't you?" Shaun had called out and before his mum got a chance to reply – we were away and out of the front door.

It was great to breathe in the fresh air of the spring day – we were both free for a while!

With Shaun still clasping me in his arms, he hurried down the drive – "Go left when you get to the pavement," I instructed him.

"Gosh, it's another large detached house," Shaun had commented as we turned into the neighbour's drive.

"Yes, it's rather a posh area you know – most of the people living in this Avenue are quite well off you know," I had informed Shaun.

"You know Matt, though mum and dad won't like me telling you this, we have just moved from a small bungalow in a village – going up in the world was mum's expression about moving here."

"Why did you move?" I had enquired.

"Mum told dad that their new neighbours had started being nasty towards her and she wanted to move, so of course dad did as he was told – he just managed to get a mortgage to afford your home, but remember I haven't told you this."

"Shaun, I never, ever tell on my friends and you are truly being one," I had replied.

The front door loomed ahead of us.

"The bell's on the right hand side of the door, Shaun," I had informed him as we approached the neighbours' door. Shaun rung the bell and waited expectantly for the door to open. I heard Henry's footsteps approaching the door before Shaun.

The tall, sturdily built figure of Henry looked down at Shaun and myself with a warm welcoming, but puzzled smile.

"Hello young man, what are you doing with my friend Matt?" Henry had enquired.

"Excuse me sir, may we come in, I need to talk to you," Shaun had politely asked.

Henry duly invited us in.

Shaun was holding me rather tightly now; I figured this must be a bit of an ordeal for him, first finding me, then having to go to a complete stranger's house and ask for help. As I listened to his words tumbling out, I was right.

"I'm very sorry to have to bother you, but we have just moved in next door to you and I don't really know how to explain this, but we, or rather I, found Matt and he asked, or rather..." Shaun stuttered as he realised that he wasn't certain who knew I could talk.

"Well, it's like this sir," Shaun stumbled even more over his words as he attempted to find a way to explain the situation.

"Just tell the truth," I whispered in his ear. "It's the simplest way."

Shaun then took a deep breath, "You see sir."

"My name's Henry by the way, young man."

"Oh, right, thanks," Shaun muttered, then added, "I'm called Shaun."

I found that I had to prompt Shaun again with yet another hurried whisper.

"You see, when we moved in mum found all this cat stuff, food, litter tray, water bowl and told my dad to throw the lot out and then I found eh, Matt upstairs and knowing that she hates cats, I thought I should

9

bring him round here and ask for your help."

I waited, almost impatiently now, for Henry's reply.

"Oh no! Are you sure Matt was actually left in the house or did he sneak in when you arrived?" Henry enquired somewhat horrified.

"No sir, eh Henry, he was definitely in the house." Shaun had finally run out of words.

Henry shook his head in disbelief, "I just cannot believe that the Robinsons would do such a thing – you'd best come through to the living room and sit down, I'll get my wife Mavis to make us a cup of tea, whilst we decide what to do."

Shaun hugging me more tightly, nervously entered.

"Don't fret Shaun," I whispered, sensing his fear. "None of this is your fault. Henry will sort it out."

Mavis being naturally curious as to what was going on, had heard most of the conversation and had taken her cue to come into the room.

"Yes, Henry I'll make us some tea, but I think the young man would prefer something different, I haven't any lemonade, but we do have some cream soda."

Mavis looked at Shaun as she spoke and watched his face light up with pleasure.

"By the way what's your name?"

"Shaun; I'd love some cream soda, it's what my grandmother always gives me."

Mavis took her cue to hurry away to make the drinks. I couldn't believe it, no one had asked me if I wanted a drink or even something to eat and I was starving by now!

Okay then – really hungry!!!

Mavis duly returned with the drinks and some chocolate biscuits – she had always believed in being hospitable.

"It's okay Matt, I haven't forgotten you, here's a bowl of water and some of your favourite crunchies, left over from the last time you stayed with us."

I was nonplussed or rather nonpussed – how could I have been so wrong, Mavis had remembered me!

"I did hear correctly didn't I, the Robinsons actually deliberately left Matt behind when they moved," Mavis stated as everyone, including me commenced eating and drinking.

"Poor old Matt, how could anyone abandon you so callously," Mavis muttered in disbelief, as she gently stroked my soft furry coat.

"Old! I'm not old," I wanted to shout, but preferring Henry and Mavis to be kept in the dark about my prowess as a talker, I managed to keep myself quiet – no mean feat, believe you me. I even let her continue to stroke me, instead of walking off in a huff, but then I was at their mercy about my future.

"Did they not leave a forwarding address with you?" enquired Shaun.

"Well done Shaun, what a brilliant question," I muttered under my breath.

"No, strangely enough they didn't," Henry and Mavis replied in unison. They didn't leave a telephone number either, nor did they own a mobile phone." Mavis stated, anticipating Shaun's next question.

I began to become restless at this point, no one seemed to be making any decisions.

Where for instance was I expected to sleep tonight.

"Could you keep him?" I heard Shaun suddenly ask.

Mavis interjected immediately, "I'm so sorry Shaun, much as we have both loved having Matt for a week or so now and then, whilst the Robinsons were on holiday, now that Henry has retired, we tend to have quite a lot of holidays, most of which are on the spur of the moment; you get some very good deals that way."

"But we can't keep him either," Shaun piped up. "Mum hates cats, though oddly she doesn't mind hamsters – I've got two of them called Jeremy and James," he stated proudly, without realizing how much

11

mental anguish was now descending upon me – no one wanted me, no one!

Suddenly Shaun looked at the pain etched on my little face and realized how unfeeling he must have appeared to me. "Can you keep Matt tonight please," he pleaded.

"Of course; we will keep him tonight and in the morning I'll ask my friend Vera if she can take Matt to an animal rescue centre she knows, they will care for him and find him a new home," Mavis stated with some relief, having made up her mind that this, in view of all the circumstances, was the most practical option opened to them.

"That will solve everyone's problem."

"Oh no! Now, not only was I not wanted, I was a problem." I wanted to scream out, yet I was stunned into a deepening silence. Shaun without warning scooped me up into his arms and hugged me so tightly I thought I was not going to be able to breathe.

"Matt, I truly think you are a great cat, but this is the only solution, please forgive me," Shaun pleaded desperately, as feelings of guilt swept over him.

"It's okay Shaun," I whispered back, "Let's part as friends." I gently licked his hand, whilst fighting to contain my fears for my future.

Shaun planted a kiss on my forehead, handed me over to Henry and then ran as fast as he could back to what was now my old home – I guessed he was crying.

Henry carried me through to their kitchen, opened a cupboard and got out my old bed they used.

"There you are Matt, you have a good sleep."

I hesitated for a moment, I really wanted to think, but then commonsense took over – I had spent two stressful days and nights and these together with all the uncertainty had taken their toll, I was truly exhausted and drained. Thus it was through sheer necessity I crept into my old bed, curled up and slept.

I woke immediately I heard the sound of a bowl hitting the tiled floor of the kitchen, it was Mavis.

"There you are Matt, it is tea time; you really were so tired you have slept all afternoon and halfway through the evening. I've also got out the litter tray from our shed."

It was a shock to realize how long I had slept – it certainly was no cat nap!

I inspected the dual bowls which I found contained tuna and water and smiled to myself, Mavis always knew what I liked, bless her. Then I remembered what I was doing there – it wasn't a break, whilst my owners were on holiday – I had been cast adrift from my past life – I would never forgive the Robinsons for such callous treatment. How could people be so cruel to animals?

I soon polished off the tuna and drank some of the water, before falling asleep again.

Wednesday 14th May

I stirred at the sound of the rain hitting the kitchen windows, it was another day and my fate was in the hands of others not mine. I instinctively miaowed for my breakfast – I was hungry. Henry and Mavis responded.

"Good morning Matt, you have had two really good sleeps."

I felt stupid, I hadn't even bothered to look around the room when I had awoken.

Mavis had already produced some food and fresh water and I eagerly tucked in and drank.

It must have been around four hours later that the doorbell rang – I watched intently as Mavis hurried through from the kitchen, across the hall and to the front door.

"Hello Vera, it is very kind of you to help us out, neither Henry or I or the new people next door could keep Matt I'm afraid; it is a reputable rescue centre isn't it?" Even as Mavis asked the question, she knew it was, but she somehow felt very guilty, because she was, in a sense, abandoning Matt too.

My ears had pricked up as I heard my name mentioned, then my heart sank as I heard the words "rescue centre" – was that to be my fate now?

"Mavis! You know full well it is," reposted Vera as she strode purposely into Mavis's kitchen.

I wanted to run and hide, better still escape and make my own new life, but as I reached the door that led from the kitchen to the garden, I saw that it was shut. Fear gripped me as I turned and watched Vera stride into the room carrying a pet carrier. I noticed the steely, no nonsense look on her face as she moved purposely towards me; one look was enough to tell me it was pointless to resist. She was one of those small thin middle aged yet getting elderly women who always got their way – the sort who were experts at using their size and demeanour to achieve this, although very few people were aware just how cold and selfish they were underneath this façade.

I instinctively shuddered as she scooped me up and popped me into the carrier – I immediately felt like the caged animal, I now was.

"Goodbye Vera and thanks again, we're both grateful for your help," Mavis called out as I watched her waving from her doorway.

I looked out through the front grill of the pet carrier saying a mental goodbye to Henry and Mavis – then as we reached the end of their drive, I caught a glimpse of Shaun standing on the pavement at the end of the drive of my now, old home.

I pressed a paw against the grill – Shaun must have seen me, because he suddenly ran towards me shouting.

"Can I just say goodbye to Matt," I heard him ask.

"Yes, but make it brief, I have lots of things to do to-day," I heard Vera snap at him, she didn't bother putting on a front with children.

"Take care Matt, I won't forget you."

"Don't worry Shaun, I'll be okay." I whispered to him as he leant down to touch me through the grill – I had to tell a white lie to reassure him, for his sake, not mine.

Vera opened the front passenger door of her car, lifted the pet carrier up and placed it in the well in front of the seat – strangely it was the place where my owners who had abandoned me, used to put me when they took me to the vets.

"Well, I should be safe here for the journey in case Vera had an accident," I consoled myself.

I soon noticed that Vera was not a bad driver, far from it; it seemed she knew that the best way to drive safely, was to treat all other road users as stupid! She actually yelled at a few as we travelled! I also noticed that Vera had the local radio station on as she drove. I knew it would let us know if there were any road traffic problems on the roads she would be taking, but where were we going? Mavis had mentioned a Rescue Centre, but how far was it from home, should I risk speaking to Vera?

"Don't," I scolded myself, "The shock will send her careering off the road! Just be patient, I'll find out when I arrive."

With that I settled down resignedly for the duration of the journey ahead of us; honestly, what else could I do?

We had been driving smoothly for over three quarters of an hour – I had heard the time given out on the radio, when suddenly the road turned into a bumpy track. It was no longer a smooth ride – if this continues I am going to be exhausted, because every time the car tyres hit another rut, I went from one side of my cage to the other and there was nothing for my little paws to hang onto either!

"Please stop soon Vera," I pleaded to myself.

Then it did stop, only this was because we had turned right and it appeared, from the sound, we were now on gravel - were we there – wherever there was?

Vera opened the passenger door.

"Out you come young man, this is now going to be your new home," she informed me as she picked up the carrier. Her thin frame belied her strength as she carried me easily across the gravelled forecourt of what was to turn out to be St.Bernard's Rescue Centre.

My head swivelled from right, then left to endeavour to take in my new surroundings. I noticed a large farmhouse with numerous outbuildings, including a reception area, shop, numerous pens of different sizes came into view and disappeared as we entered the reception area.

"Hello Vera, how are you?" came the warm and genuine greeting from the young girl, stationed behind the reception desk.

"Fine thanks, Jill."

Jill was to turn out to be a Jill of all trades, in that her main occupation was really tending to the wide variety of animals which were brought to St.Bernard's.

"Hmm, St.Bernard's – surely that means that they take in dogs as well. My initial fear of the place, was now being taken over by curiosity.

"I see you have brought me another cat," Jill added as Vera deposited the pet carrier on the counter.

"Yes, his name is Matt – for some reason he was left alone in his owners' house when they moved out."

"Oh, Vera, how can people be so uncaring, to just abandon an animal in that way. I have never been able to comprehend some people's actions. I guess we just have to accept that there are some truly rotten people out there, who are just utterly thoughtless and cruel."

I listened intently as the conversation continued, after all, my future was going to be decided in this place.

"Yes, there are – I call them Yobs, regardless of their age," Vera replied.

I watched as Jill crossed to a cabinet and removed a form from a file. It turned out to be my admittance form and I watched and listened as she filled in the form very quickly, until it had my name, Matt, colouring, breed and age unknown written down.

"I'm sorry Jill, I really must go, I brought Matt out here as a favour to some friends and if I leave any later I will get caught up in the commuter traffic near my home."

So, without so much as a goodbye to me or even a pat, Vera strode –

she wasn't the type of woman you could say walked – out of reception.

My curiosity immediately vanished with Vera's departure, I was feeling petrified now – first there had been the two nights alone at home, then the night at Henry and Mavis's home and now I had been abandoned for the third time – only it was at a Rescue Centre. In my short life I had never heard of them, did it mean someone would rescue me, or was the Centre or Jill my rescuer? The grill of the carrier was opened and I was grabbed gently by the scruff of my neck and deposited on the counter, before I could even put up a struggle.

Now what, I wondered.

I felt Jill's hands parting and examining my fur – so it was flea inspection time! Then my mouth was opened, teeth inspected, ears inspected, eyes inspected, tail lifted – what next. Of course, I had been inspected at a Vet's before, but it felt undignified here.

"Well young Matt, despite whatever made your owners abandon you, you appear to be in good health, but you will have to go into one of the isolation pens until the Vet has been to see you, though I am now going to apply some preventative flea treatment before his inspection."

After this, Jill picked me up, "Here we go again," I thought as Jill took me outside and carried me towards a line of pens, then I saw the sign - isolation pens! Jill opened, entered and then locked the main gate, then a pen was opened and Jill, I must say, gently put me on the ground, before closing and locking the pen.

Without warning I started to tremble – I was truly alone and I needed a friend – I made a decision, a brave one out of the overwhelming sense of hopelessness.

"Jill, I feel so alone, will you be my friend?"

Jill swung round in amazement, "You can talk Matt!"

"Yes, but can it be our secret please" I replied.

"Of course and I will be your friend – I'll bring you some fresh food and water in a few minutes and then you can settle down for the night."

Jill's voice was soothing and I felt the ring of honesty in her voice too, so I waited patiently until she returned with my food and water.

17

"You are a very kind young lady to a stranger in your midst," I told her with a gentle smile. "I just feel so alone."

"Oh Matt", she answered, picking me up and cuddling me.

How could she have known how much I needed a cuddle.

After Jill had left and I had refreshed myself with the food and water, I then noticed that there was a small cubby hole at the back of the pen – it was a kennel.

I was now so tired, I decided to climb in, bed myself down and go to sleep.

"See you in the morning world," I said courageously; it was bravado I know, but it would get me through yet another night.

Thursday 15th May

I was woken by the rattling of the pen being open this morning, in fact I actually stirred lazily, for I had had a good night's sleep. It was only when I looked around and realized where I was that I suddenly sat bolt upright and fully awake. Before I had time to fully gather my senses an unfamiliar, but friendly voice said,

"Hello Matt."

I looked up expecting to see Jill, but it was another young girl, well at least she had got my name correct.

"Don't look so puzzled Matt, she said, "Your name is on the front of the gate to your pen."

"Hmm, this one could read my thoughts, best be careful," I told myself.

"I'm Angela should you wish to know, I guess you must have been expecting to see Jill again. I shall be looking after you now, whilst you get settled in here."

"Settled in, how long was I expected to stay here?" I wondered.

"I hope you like your food in jelly? I have also brought you some crunchies – they are very nutritious and good for your teeth young man, plus fresh water," she informed me as she put the food down inside the pen. I observed that she had carefully closed the pen gate behind her as she entered. No escape then!

"Well, at least I do like my food in jelly," I muttered to myself as I looked up at Angela. She was a jolly looking girl, shortish, with rich dark hair that just touched her shoulders, stocky too, which I reckoned came from a lot of hard physical work in the open air, I liked her.

Angela gave me a warm smile, as she bent down to stroke me. I welcomed the stroking as much as the food – it made me feel that someone cared and I was in need of any form of reassurance. Angela stayed with me for a while as she tidied up the pen, not that there was much to do in that way – let's face it I had only been here a night!

Perhaps it would be a better day, I felt I deserved a good day, after all didn't dogs have them. My mates had often told me this – the thought disturbed me, as it dawned that I would probably never see them again.

"Come on Matt," I told myself, "To-day was going to be a better day, remember."

Angela then got out her cat comb and reached out to comb me. I instinctively backed away. I didn't mind her stroking or feeding me, but I was just wary of being combed. Although the Robinsons had been good owners, I had hated the way they had combed me so much, that I would often twist and turn and scratch them. Was this why they had abandoned me?

"It's okay Matt, I only want to comb your fur, it keeps you from getting too many fur balls, which can make you sick and besides it makes you look good. The Vet should be visiting you to-day," she then added.

"Vet, why on earth do I need a Vet? I knew I had had a rough few days and nights, but I wasn't ill," I muttered under my breath.

Angela sensed my reluctance at the news and explained that all new boarders had to have a medical by the Vet from Woodley Green, a nearby village. I noted that like all cat and animal lovers, Angela talked to them – what a huge surprise she would have had, if I had told her that I actually understood every word she was saying., well apart from those I had never heard before. It would have been an even bigger

19

surprise if I had made the decision to talk to her.

Angela reached out once more to comb me and I decided, with reluctance to let her as I remembered how it felt being sick with fur balls. Not a pleasant experience.

Her work duly completed Angela patted me and said,

"See you later Matt" and with those parting words, she gave me another smile and went jauntily on her way, locking the pen gate behind her – curses, she was efficient too!

I decided to eat my refreshments which, being an honest cat, were quite palatable.

In fact I polished off the food surprisingly quickly, despite having been fed well last night.

Afterwards I sat outside my little kennel and leisurely groomed myself; like all cats, I was fastidious at keeping myself clean. I then walked to the front of the pen and looked out across the path dividing my row of pens from those opposite. I could see other cats in the pens – had we all been abandoned? I looked up to see what was above me, only to find that the 'roof' of my pen was also made of mesh, like the sides and front, although my gate had metal bars. Above the mesh was a proper roof to keep out the rain, although a glass skylight ran the length of the path letting in daylight, I shuddered, let's face it, I was in prison.

"Hello young fellow, what are you in for?" Came a jovial query from the pen on my left.

"Nothing, I haven't committed any crime," I retorted annoyed and surprised at the question.

"Are you sure?" Said my neighbour teasingly.

"Look, I am entirely innocent; I was abandoned – that's all."

"We all are my friend, that's why we're here. Sorry you took offence, I was only teasing. My name is Tom, as in Tomcat! Guess my owners must have had a sense of humour," he finished.

"Sorry, I was rude, but I have had a truly horrible few days – my owners moved house and just left me behind," I informed him. "My name's Matt."

"Matt the Cat, what a great name – my owner died and none of her family wanted me. In the end a nephew brought me here and left," Tom continued. "Most of us have been abandoned one way or another. Tammy on your right hand side was brought in after spending days trying to get taken in by another family, but they were very hard hearted – kept telling her to go away; wouldn't even feed her, but when she didn't, a friend of theirs brought her here too," Tom concluded.

"Do you know what happens now?" I asked.

"We're all waiting for the Vet – we're all in isolation until he gives us a clean bill of health – then we are allowed into the bigger pens with the other cats," Tom continued.

"Then what?" I queried.

"That's when you stand a chance of finding a new home – visitors wanting a pet come and look us over."

"How do you know all this, when you are in isolation yourself," I asked suspiciously.

"Via the catvine of course," Tom laughed.

"We're all rescued cats, one way or another," Tammy, who had been listening to our conversation piped up.

The three of us cattered for a while – come on, it's people who chatter, we catter!

The catter over, I started to console myself with the hope that I would be chosen quickly. I might have feline company, but I needed to be loved by a human, for I loved being stroked, cuddled, needed and wanted, which is why I found it so hurtful to have been abandoned.

I looked down the path to the main gate and noticed the sky was overcast, but at least it wasn't raining, not that I could get out and at least I did have shelter.

The morning passed and I was getting bored.

"Just when is the Vet coming?" I asked Tom.

"Very soon," he replied. "Just be patient."

It was mid afternoon when the main gate suddenly swung open and Mr. Harmer, the Vet strode briskly and purposely in, followed by Angela.

Then my pen gate was opened.

"Let's have a look at you young man," he said as he picked me up and put me onto the portable table that Angela had brought with her.

I watched curiously as Angela got out her clip board, ready to take down my details, I figured. She duly informed the Vet that I had been given the preventative flea treatment on arrival.

"Right, well he is definitely male and he has been neutered. Ears – fine, eyes – nice and clear, now let's have a look at your mouth and check your teeth; no problems there – good. Legs and paws – okay my friend there's no need to get frightened, you can put those claws away now."

Reluctantly, I obeyed.

"Nothing wrong, so far – age I should say about two years old, although of course you cannot really tell a cat's exact age. Breed – unknown, but interesting colouring, quite striking really. Let's take your temperature now shall we."

It was a statement, not a question.

I had had my temperature taken before and had hated it, in fact no cat I knew had ever looked forward to this being done.

"Why couldn't cats have their temperatures taken as humans do," I pondered.

I was also angry and annoyed, I knew Tom had informed me about the clean bill of health business, but I hadn't thought it would be this thorough.

"Temperature, normal – I see Matt was brought in by Vera, I would be grateful Angela, if you could check with her to see if she can find out from the neighbours as to whether he has been wormed regularly and if he has also been vaccinated and if so, how long ago; get back to me when you have all the details please. Brief history – abandoned. Well that's all for this visit young man," stated Mr. Harmer, then he gave me a gentle pat as he put me back onto the floor of the pen, before walking off just as briskly as he had arrived to the next pen.

"Look out Tom, I whispered, "You're next."

Angela quickly shut the gate to my pen and began washing down the examination table ready for Tom.

Mr. Harmer however, only stayed very briefly with Tom; in fact as I watched, he was only given an injection. Mr. Harmer then left Tom's pen and went past my pen to visit Tammy, who to amazement, also only had an injection.

"Something's odd here," I told myself. "Why didn't they get the full treatment like me?"

I then remembered a favourite quotation of a dear friend, "If you want to know anything, just ask."

"Goodbye Mr. Harmer and thanks; see you next week," Angela called out as the Vet left the pen.

I watched Mr. Harmer leave – he was as meticulous as Angela – yes, he locked the main pen gate too!

Angela returned to my pen.

"There Matt, that wasn't too bad; I'm afraid all the new strays have to be examined thoroughly, as we cannot have you spreading any diseases to the other animals Once you have been checked out and sorted regarding the worming and vaccination you will be able to mix with the other cats in the main pen – you will be happier then. I'm off now, but don't fret, I'll be back with your evening meal and see you, Tom and Tammy all settled in for the night."

I watched as Angela duly left, yet again, carefully locking my pen and then the main pen gate as well as taking the table away with her.

"Tom, Tammy, what is going on?" I urgently enquired as soon as Angela disappeared from sight.

"What do you mean Matt?" they both responded.

"How come I got the full treatment, whilst you two only just had an injection each?"

I stated, trying to keep the annoyance out of my voice.

"I'm sorry Matt, but I didn't want to worry you by giving you all the details of the procedures we have to go through in the isolation pen – it would only have made you anxious," responded Tom.

"Tammy felt the same way, so we both kept quiet."

"I would have preferred to have been told the truth, it's less painful in the end," I found myself snapping back. I hated subterfuge.

"Look it up in a dictionary, if you don't understand, it's the best way to increase your vocabulary." Gosh, I was angry, as I listened to my own voice!

"Sorry Matt, we didn't mean to make you angry – we both only had one injection as it was our last part of the treatment," Tom explained, apologizing for himself and Tammy.

I never could stay angry for long, so I accepted their apology.

I learnt later, via the catvine, that after Angela had stored the table, she had returned to the reception area to inform Jill of the Vet's comments and request her to check with Vera to see if she could find out the necessary information – as I knew Jill had Vera's telephone number, I hoped it would not be a long wait.

Apparently then, Jill and Angela got started on their individual tasks – Angela on her rounds and Jill, contacting Vera so she could settle me quickly in the 'family pen.' Jill told me later that she preferred any newcomers to spend as little time as possible on their own, especially as most of us had been through various kinds of trauma before arriving at the Centre.

Apparently, I was to discover, I wasn't the exception – I was the rule.

Our evening meal duly arrived and yet again we all settled down later, for another night, but I did remember my manners and said goodnight to both Tom and Tammy.

"I suppose you could call us The Three Catastrophes." I stated and waited.

Sure enough the groans of Tom and Tammy echoed around at my terrible pun!

"Goodnight Matt!" had come the joint reply, "Anymore like that and we won't speak to you in the morning."

But of course they would!

Friday 16th May

This day passed by with very little happening, apart from being fed and groomed.

Saturday 17th May

Yet another dull, boring day, except word got round that it was visitors' day. Whatever that meant.

Sunday 18th May

A whole week had now passed since I was abandoned.

I later heard this was another visitors' day and had discovered these were two of the days visitors came to look us over as a possible pet – this appeared to be the only way out of St. Bernard's, unless you managed to escape!

Monday 19th May

"Hello Matt," my ears pricked up as I heard the friendly voice of Jill – great I could talk to her, only she had come to talk to me.

"Your friend Vera telephoned to-day and apologized for the delay – she has had a word with your neighbours, Henry and Mavis, but unfortunately neither of them have any knowledge about your medical history, in fact they even checked with their new neighbours in case the Robinsons had left any details concerning you behind when they moved, but there was absolutely nothing. That's why I haven't been to see you earlier, se we will just have to deal with you in the normal way now."

"What's the normal way Jill," I enquired, wondering what was coming next.

"The Vet has to start from scratch, that's all – nothing to worry about Matt, truly,"

Jill patted me, smiled and left.

Well, that was a brief visit," now I had something else to ponder on – "What was the normal way and what did starting from scratch mean."

I decided to ask Tom and Tammy, because if their recent injection was the last part of their treatment, they must know what preceded this.

I called out to Tom, "Jill has just informed me that they are starting from scratch with me and as you said on Thursday you had just had your last part of the treatment, could you now explain – please tell me the truth this time," I pleaded.

"You see, Tom if people and animals would fully explain matters in the first place, I wouldn't spend my time fretting."

"It's not complicated Matt, you have already been examined, now it's just a bit of treatment."

Tom was hedging when there was really no need.

"Are you going to tell me please," I persisted.

"Okay, it's just a tablet and injections – you'll see, just be patient Matt, came the nondescript reply.

This made me decide to give up trying to get a more detailed explanation and just wait.

I was now beginning to hate my solitary pen and lack of a human owner, especially the cuddles. I also hated the state of being trapped in an unfamiliar world. I had thought of making a bolt through the pen's gate, the previous evening when Angela had brought my evening meal, but it would have been futile, because even if I had managed to slip past her, Angela, as I had already observed was meticulous in locking all the gates behind her as she entered and left.

Also I was a freedom loving creature; it was summer and I wanted to be outdoors exploring and lazing in the warmth of the sun – I might be safe here, but I wasn't living. The day and evening passed, uneventful as usual.

Tuesday 20th May

Another day of waiting – when was the Vet coming again?

Wednesday 21st May

Yet another day of waiting and solitary confinement – I was just grateful I had Tom and Tammy to talk to – not that there was really much to discuss – we were all in a state of suspension really.

Thursday 22nd May

Jill had popped in briefly during the morning to tell me that the Vet was coming in the afternoon – perhaps now my life would start to move forward.

Mr. Harmer duly arrived mid afternoon along with Angela carrying the examination table.

"I've already been examined, there's nothing wrong with me," I wanted to scream at both of them, out of fear and frustration.

"Hold him firmly, please Angela," Mr. Harmer instructed her. I was now in a firm, but inescapable grip.

"Nothing to worry about; as you are classified as a stray and we've been unable to trace your medical records, we have to start from scratch."

"I can scratch too," I wanted to shout at him, but of course I kept quiet.

"So, first Matt, I want you to swallow this tablet, it's a worming tablet for cats, it will protect you from worms, that is round worms, hook worms and tape worms."

Before I could take in all this information, he had opened my mouth wide, popped a tablet into it and then held my mouth shut tight – I can tell you I wasn't happy with this, as I swallowed automatically. As I did so I remembered I had had this done before and hadn't liked it then. For my pains, Mr. Harmer gave me a solitary pat.

"Make a note that his next dose will be in three months time."

I was watching Mr. Harmer intently now as he reached into his case and drew out a syringe unwrapped it and proceeded to fill it from a small bottle.

"Oh, here we go, injection time," I said under my breath as Angela's grip tightened.

"Ready; here we go Matt."

I only felt a slight prick as the needle entered my body – it hadn't hurt really, but all the same I was relieved when the needle was removed.

"That's one Primary Vaccination against enteritis and Cat's flu, date 22nd May, Angela. I'll be back in three weeks' time for Matt's second dose, which acts as a booster to this one, if you could just put that on his records too please," Mr. Harmer stated, as he gave me another pat. "Bye young man, don't worry, a week after the second injection you will be able to join the other cats in the main pen – you'll be happier then. Bye Angela," he added and duly left to complete his rounds.

"Four more weeks of solitary," I was hurt, angry and felt a pang of despair at this news.

After Mr. Harmer had finally left, Tom and I catter about my predicament, but neither of us could really comfort the other. His predicament was different. To be honest, I wanted to curl up and cry; it was so unfair and there was nothing to be done, except wait.

Angela came round later with our evening meal and sensed my mood. She actually stroked me gently to reassure me.

"You won't be on your own much longer – these injections have to be done to protect you and the other animals – the time will soon pass, honestly."

"What a big fib, you should try being in solitary confinement," I wanted to shout, instead I watched Angela leave, with tears welling up in my eyes, I just felt so utterly lonely – I let out a plaintive soft howl, climbed into my cubby hole and wept.

Friday 23rd May

Tom and Tammy left the solitary confinement pens to-day – it was now a week since their final injection. They were both naughty in not having explained everything fully to me however, we said our goodbyes as friends and Tom apologized yet again for not being completely honest.

"I was doing my best to protect you," was his excuse!

Saturday 24th May to Wednesday 11th June

The days passed slowly by and I continued to miss being outside playing in the garden, lazing on the lawn in the sunshine back home even more. I wondered how Tom and Tammy were faring in the main pen, would they even be there when it was my time to rejoin them? Angela still fed me regularly, but life was very dull and boring, except for the 11th June when Angela came as usual with my evening meal.

"You will be pleased to know that Mr. Harmer is coming tomorrow to give you the booster – then Matt, just think, one more week after that and you will be able to join the other cats in the main pen – Tom and Tammy are still there at the moment. I noticed she was watching my face intently as she gave me this information. I looked up and gave her a beaming smile – a true Matt the Cat smile.

"There I knew you would be pleased."

That night I ate and slept well.

Thursday 12th June

I woke early and spent most of the morning and early afternoon impatiently pacing up and down my pen.

"Matt," I told myself, "it doesn't matter how much you pace up and down, Mr. Harmer will not get here any earlier."

I knew this of course, but I had to do something to occupy my mind and being caged up, I was limited in my choices of things to do, but sometimes in life you have to keep moving; it was certainly better than just sitting there – it really was a form of distraction exercise and I consoled myself with this thought.

Tom, I knew was lucky; he was a very laid back patient cat. I doubted if anything or anyone could ever disturb his placid nature.

Then I saw Mr. Harmer approaching with Angela in tow.

"Okay Matt, it is only one more injection to-day and then one more week and you can leave the solitary confinement of this pen and join the others – you will have plenty of company then," the reassuring voice of Mr. Harmer had spoken.

Angela held me firmly, but I was fine, I knew what was happening this time.

"All done, Matt – that's the last injection – you will only need a booster once a year now," Mr. Harmer stated, giving me another of his comforting friendly pats as he left.

I was now pleased and couldn't wait to meet the other cats – with apologies in advance to Tom and Tammy, it had been a long while since I had had an intelligent conversation, perhaps I would find one in the main pen.

I hadn't been bosom pals with Trixie (why did all my cat friends' names begin with a 'T'), who lived a few doors away when I was at home in the Avenue, but at least she had been reasonably knowledgeable

Strange, this was the first time I had actually thought about her since I had been abandoned. This thought led me down the path of thinking about the Robinsons, who so cruelly had abandoned me. To be truthful, it was something I really didn't want to consider – it was still too raw and painful. I only wished there was someone who would take me away from this awful predicament I found myself in.

Friday 13th June

I had no problem with this date – I had never been superstitious, in fact I made a point of walking under ladders!

Saturday 14th June to Wednesday 18th June

These days were warm and humid, during my last week in the isolation pen, so knowing I would soon have the company of Tom, Tammy and a whole new group of other cats, I made the most of these days by spending them lying outside my small kennel enjoying the sunshine shining through the glass panel and dreaming of better times to come. Though I had another flea treatment on the 14th.

Thursday 19th June

"Hello Matt, it's time to join the others," so saying Angela scooped me up and carried me out of the pen that had been my home for practically five weeks. My little heart began to race, but not through fear, just sheer relief; happiness surged through my whole body, I was leaving the isolation pens! I had no one to say goodbye to, as there had not been any new arrivals during Tom and Tammy's absence, so I just whispered silently "Goodbye pens, I'm on my way."

At least now, I felt I would be getting closer to having contact with the real world. Angela duly locked the door of my solitary confinement pen behind her, carried me to the main gate, unlocked it and walked through, then turned round to lock it behind her. Meticulous as ever.

I was getting really excited now – something positive was actually happening – I wouldn't feel so lonely anymore – during the next few minutes my life would begin a new phase. I welcomed the challenge, even though deep down, I admitted to myself, I was really rather nervous, but my dearest friend had once told me I was a fighter and survivor and I became determined to live up to his memory of me.

It was quite a walk to the large main cat pen, but I spent the time enjoying being cuddled in Angela's arms. She really should have put me in a pet carrier, but I guess she knew I would enjoy the cuddle.

We duly arrived. Angela unlocked the outer gate of the main cat pen, again locking it behind her, before opening the actual gate to the main pen.

She slowly lowered me onto the concrete surface of the main pen, gently patted me and said,

"Off you go Matt and meet the others." Then she left.

Suddenly, I felt vulnerable, for let's face it, I was very much 'the new

31

cat on the block,' in fact I was now very conscious of being given the once over by at least eighteen other cats and I couldn't see either Tom or Tammy. At this stage, I'm afraid I actually froze on the spot, but although I felt I couldn't move, I was slowly taking in my new surroundings. The pen was very large compared to my previous one. There were sheets of newspapers scattered around the floor and there appeared to be a large opening on the far right hand side of the pen. I was curious now.

Gingerly, I walked around my new territory eyeing each of the other cats in turn, yet still looking for Tom and Tammy.

I had to admit, I had never seen such a variety of breeds and sizes all at the same time. A strikingly large grey fluffy cat gave me a half welcoming smile as I slowly strolled past – I smiled in return.

"Contact at long last," I sighed with some relief." Perhaps the others would be friendly too."

I must have spent about twenty minutes checking on my new quarters and the other cats, but still no Tom or Tammy. I padded over to the large opening I had spotted earlier and entered into a large living room, where I discovered quite a few other cats lounging in armchairs or curled up on settees. Suddenly a voice called out.

"Hello Matt, welcome to your new abode." It was Tom.

My heart soared. I ran eagerly over to greet him and ask where Tammy was, as I still hadn't seen her. Tom's answer didn't really surprise me

"Tammy was taken very quickly, in fact on the first visitors' day we had, whilst she was here. She was a very attractive cat, as you know with lovely fur and colouring – that's what some people go for – looks, not character," he ended. Gosh, how I envied her.

"I'm sorry I missed her departure, I would have liked to said goodbye to her properly," I responded.

I then noticed all the lounging cats were eyeing me with typical curiosity and the curiosity didn't kill them – as humans are always stating!!! Some were looking with sympathy too, after all we were all in the same pen, although for many varied reasons I was to find, yet with the same dream of finding a loving owner and new home. I, for the moment, was just basically glad to be amongst fellow cats and back with Tom.

I strolled back outside, into the sunshine, with Tom for company. I was pleased all this was happening to me during the summer months – at least even here I could stretch out in the sun – I loved sunbathing and feeling the warmth of the sun on my body. The skylights in the isolation pens really didn't allow this.

Tom began introducing me to some of the cats, but to be honest, I suddenly felt hungry and wondered from which bowl I could or should eat, for there was plenty of food and water bowls dotted around the pen.

Tom spotted me looking longingly at the food bowls.

"It's okay Matt, just eat."

Thus encouraged I started on the food bowl nearest and despite Tom's reassuring words, was pleasantly surprised when none of the other cats objected or stopped me, so I satisfied my hunger – realizing I hadn't had any breakfast. I also had a long drink.

Feeling more refreshed and confident now, I continued on my conducted tour with Tom.

"Hi, what happened to you then?"

I stopped at the sound of the friendly voice and explained in some detail, the story of my misfortune, to the enquiring black and white cat.

"I feel for you, Matt – I was just taken for a long drive and dumped in the countryside – I've stopped feeling sorry for myself though; you just want to hear some of the other cats' stories. Squidge over there, along with five other cats, was rescued from a house where the owner was found to no longer have the ability to look after them – the state they were all in was appalling. Ben, that black cat in the corner was in the act of being drowned when a young man rescued him."

I listened intently as the running commentary continued about the other occupants.

"What terrible stories; my name's Matt," thinking it was about time I introduced myself, "What's your name?" I politely enquired.

"Tiddlywinks," he replied.

Without thinking I found myself laughing out loud.

"Why?" I asked, as I apologized for my laughter.

"It's okay Matt, everyone else laughs when I tell them. The children of the thoughtless parents, who dumped me in the countryside, were always playing the game and it was on my name tag attached to my collar."

Changing the subject, I asked, "How long do the cats normally spend here?"

"Depends Matt – if you are handsome or beautiful, you could be out of here in a week," Tiddlywinks replied.

"A week!" I echoed delightedly.

"Yes, it depends on so many things though, some cats just click with certain people. I'm afraid some of us have been here for months, though through no fault of their own," Tiddlywinks concluded.

I cringed in horror at the thought of being in captivity for months, but then remembered that I, with my striking black, deep ginger, brown and white markings, was quite a colourful cat, surely someone would pick me quickly, especially if I gave them one of my beaming smiles.

"Mind you," continued Tiddlywinks, "It's summer now and that helps a lot – you see people go out more in their cars, especially to the countryside where we are based, also the rescue centre is open more often and longer, because of the length of the daylight hours, hence more visitors." He reiterated.

"How long do you think I'll be here then," I asked.

"Depends, you're not really handsome are you, so I should make up for it by being extra friendly to anyone who approaches you," came Tiddlywinks somewhat blunt reply.

"Does it work?" I asked still stunned by his reply. I hadn't expected him to make such a direct remark, especially as I had always thought of myself as striking.

"Sorry I was so rude; actually you are rather striking in a way," Tiddlywinks continued. "Look just be nice to the visitors, approach them first, rather than wait for them to come to you, they appreciate that; you see quite a few of them have just lost man's best friend.

"I though dogs were suppose to be man's best friend," Tom who had been listening butted in.

"They were for far longer than us cats care to remember, but recently when Angela and some of the other staff were laying down fresh newspapers, I read an article that stated that cat owners now outnumbered dog owners, so I reckon WE are now man's best friends," Tiddlywinks replied emphasizing the WE.

"That will put some dogs' noses out of joint," I replied.

"Mine you, I remember my dad telling me, not to believe everything you read, half of what you see and nothing of what you hear!" Tiddlywinks added by way of a footnote.

"That's rather a cynical view point," stated Tom, who had been silently listening to our conversation.

"Possibly, but it's mine!" Tiddlywinks emphasized. "By the way, there's no one here you need be afraid of," he continued still feeling he had to somehow make it up to me for his bluntness.

"Thanks," I had wondered."

"Come on, I noticed Tom here introducing you to some of the cats, I'll introduce you to some more of them, you will feel a lot happier then."

Tiddlywinks might be blunt, but he was also kind.

I was grateful for his offer and thus spent the rest of my first day in the pen getting to know the other cats, with Tiddlywinks and Tom.

Our evening meal duly arrived with Angela and two other young ladies dispensing the food amongst us in fresh bowls, after which they collected up the morning's bowls for washing. We were all tucking in, before they had even left.

It had been a better day than I had dared hope. Practically all the other cats were friendly, but then we were all very much in the same predicament – wondering just how long it would be before someone decided they might just be the pet they were searching for.

I didn't, of course, know how long it would take, but I made a promise to myself, that whatever happened I would endeavour to use all my wiles to obtain a new beginning for myself.

I watched the sun setting, it's light creating streaks of a red/orange hue across the deepening blue sky as the day gradually drew to a close and along with the other cats we all retired into, what I learnt they called 'the lounge' – thus ending my first day amongst my 'new family' in the main pen – real company at last with no catty ones amongst them!

Friday 20th June

I stirred, ears pricking up immediately, along with the other cats, as soon as I heard the outer door to the main pen being opened. It was then closed and locked.

"Does no one ever forget to lock the doors around here," I enquired of Tom, who was nearby. "Has anyone ever managed to escape from the main pen? I continued.

Tiddlywinks interrupted, before Tom could give a response to my question.

"NO," came his emphatic reply.

My heart sank momentarily, but then the inner door opened and along with all the other cats in the pen I was instead waiting eagerly – it was morning – food was coming.

A slim, tall lady, with long blonde hair tied back in a pony tail entered our inner sanctum, pulling behind her a trailer loaded with bowls of fresh food and drinking water. She was accompanied by another young lady, somewhat shorter, with a round face and short dark hair.

"Who are they?" I enquired of the nearest cat.

"You must be the new cat Matt, it you don't know Susan," came the reply. "She's the one with the long blonde hair and her friend is Rachel – they were with Angela last night. They normally do the morning shift. I'm Mitzi in case you are wondering. I watched Tom and Tiddlywinks giving you the conducted tour yesterday; it will take you a while to remember all our names – it's easier for us, we only have to remember yours."

"Very true – I'm afraid I wasn't taking that much notice of them yesterday." Having finished my brief conversation with Mitzi, I sat watching intently as Susan and Rachel carefully began dispensing the bowls from the trailer around the pen, whilst at the same time gathering up the previous night's bowls. I was impressed and pleased to note the attention to good food hygiene. I had always felt rather sorry for Trixie, whose owners sometimes only cleaned her bowls every other day. For a moment, I wondered whether Trixie missed me or even knew what had happened to me; it was now over a month since I had been abandoned. I didn't even know if any of the cats in my old neighbourhood had even seen me taken away by Vera – then I remembered Shaun and the sadness returned.

"Snap out of it Matt," I told myself. "Don't dwell on the past – you cannot change it; the most important thing concerning your life right now is in the future, so direct your thoughts in that direction, besides breakfast is here."

I snapped out of my reverie to find that all the cats were by now, tucking into their breakfast; I joined them gratefully, after all I had my health, company again and I was being properly looked after at St. Bernard's. Tiddlywinks strolled over to see me as soon as he had finished his meal; he was still feeling guilty about his rather brutal remark the previous day.

"Hello Matt, I trust you are enjoying your breakfast?" he enquired in his friendliest voice.

I looked up from my bowl, pleasantly surprised that he had sought out my company so early in the day. I was doubly pleased, because now I could clear up some outstanding points with him.

"Tiddlywinks, would you mind if I asked you how long you have been here?" I enquired tentatively.

"No, I'm surprised that you didn't raise the question yesterday," came the reply. "To the best of my knowledge I've been here just over seven weeks – at times I must admit it has seemed a lot longer though," Tiddlywinks sighed.

"Have you or any of the others tried to escape," I enquired hopefully.

Tiddlywinks laughed – "It's wishful thinking Matt, so you can forget about escaping. I told you yesterday that no one had ever escaped. I myself asked Ben, over there and some of the others the same question when I was put in here. No one apparently has ever escaped; the staff are very security conscious – you must surely have noticed that when you were in quarantine?"

"Yes, I did," I replied rather crestfallen. "I just wondered if anyone had ever tried, that's all."

"Come on Matt cheer up, no one wants to take home a miserable looking cat – you have to learn to stay as cheerful as possible, not only will it boost your morale, but the other cats pick up on each other's moods and the visitors always seem to sense this too," Tiddlywinks stated very firmly.

I was going to have to learn fast if I wanted a new owner and I realized Tiddlywinks had wanted to make absolutely certain that I was aware of this fact.

"It's okay, I take your point." I replied. "When do the visitors normally arrive?"

"Anytime after 11 a.m. to-day - Saturday, Sunday and midweek, that's to allow for everyone to be fed, groomed and the pens cleaned and the newspapers changed in the toilet areas, plus of course the litter trays," Tiddlywinks replied. "We also normally close at 5.00 p.m. this time of year," he added by way of further information.

I returned to my breakfast rather disappointed – I would have to wait another day before the visitors came.

Later, I strolled over to join Tom, who was busy washing himself, so I sat down beside him and began to groom myself too –appearance was important, if you are going to make an impression – even in the cat world.

After a while two other cats joined us – I wondered whether I should speak first, but the decision was taken out of my hands as Tom suddenly spoke.

"Matt, this is Mr. Tibbs and his friend Lulubelle – they were brought in, some weeks ago, after their owner died and none of her relatives wanted them."

Mr. Tibbs, I observed was a tabby, whereas Lulubelle's fur was a beautiful soft ginger colour. Together they made such an interesting and contrasting pair that I couldn't understand why no one had adopted them immediately.

"I can see you are wondering why we are still here, Matt," Mr. Tibbs boldly stated.

"Well yes, I was actually – how on earth did you know?" I answered somewhat astounded.

"I could tell from your face, Matt – we are still here, because very few people who visit want two cats and Lulubelle and I have no intention or desire to be separated and thankfully the staff of St. Bernard's follow a policy of not separating cats who have been brought up together by their previous owner," Mr. Tibbs explained.

"Thanks for the information. I hope you both soon find an owner or owners who will give you the same amount of love and care that you both obviously have for each other," I sympathetically replied.

"Thanks, Matt – that is a very kind observation," piped up Lulubelle, determined not to be left out of the conversation.

Then Susan returned along with Rachel to comb us all and clean the pen, thus putting an end to our conversation.

We then all spent the next part of the morning, continuing with washing and doing our best to look as smart and appealing as possible before 11 a.m.

"They're here," shouted Tom excitedly as the first visitors of the day could be seen walking towards our pen. A buzz of anticipation ran amongst us as everyone heard Tom call out. I wondered if it was like this every day the visitors came and decided it was, for without hope there is nothing left. With this thought uppermost in my mind, I gave myself a quick final groom.

I decided to position myself well away from the gate into the pen, or the house as I shall now call my temporary home, rather than immediately approach the first people who entered. My commonsense told me that anyone looking for a new pet would want to study all the cats first, before deciding which one to choose and I knew my pride would be hurt, if I was one of the first to be studied and then ignored. It was then, I noticed, that Tom was watching from a distance too.

Even though the first wave of visitors to the house turned out to be just seven people, they seemed to make the house shrink in size and I began to feel hemmed in and nervous. Tom sidled up to me.

"Don't be so nervous Matt, No one is going to hurt you," he muttered softly by way of reassurance.

"But they are," I replied. "You see each group of visitors that come and leave without me is a rejection and it's not something I have experienced before or want to go through on a regular basis."

"Matt, some of us have been 'rejected' as you call it, loads of times, it is something you just have got to get use to and accept – the only thing you mustn't do, is take it personally. Everyone who comes here has a preconceived idea of the cat they are looking for, be it breed, age, colour, size and overall appearance. If none of us are chosen – it's just because, what they are looking for is not here, do you understand?"

"Yes, thanks Tom, I do, but all the same I'm going to stay here and observe the comings and goings" I answered. "Some people though just fall in love at first sight – that is possible you know," I concluded.

"You're a romantic," Tom smiled back amused at my statement.

"Yes, always have been," I responded with a grin.

The two couples who had entered the house first, were busy observing all of us from a distance, whereas the three young children with them were going from one cat to another stroking and patting each one in turn. I watched fascinated.

"Mum, dad, what do you think of this one?" came the call as one of the children picked up Ben. "Aren't black cats suppose to be lucky?"

"Yes, Jason they are – do you want a black cat then?" his mum asked, somewhat surprised that for once her offspring seemed to be making a quick decision.

"Yes, can we take him then?" answered Jason, now hugging Ben close to his little chest.

"Of course you can," stated his relieved mum, who could now leave the house quickly.

The moment she had entered the house, all she could feel was sadness for all the cats there, knowing that they had all been deserted, for whatever reason by their previous owner.

I had watched her closely when she first entered the house and noticed the involuntarily shudder she gave, when she observed just how many there were of us. I continued watching as they left the pen, thinking that Ben was a lucky cat, but then realized that Ben had been left behind and this perplexed me.

I padded over for a brief chat, "Hey Ben, that was quick, you are lucky, but why have they left you behind?"

"Matt, I was as flabbergasted as you at first," he breathlessly replied. "Apparently though, they cannot take you home immediately – first they have to put a deposit on their chosen cat and then return a few days later to collect it – this process gives the new owner the opportunity to change their mind before committing themselves, after which the staff here check out the prospective owners. Even homes are inspected in some cases. I then have to be microchipped before I leave."

"Microchipped, what on earth is that?"

"To be honest Matt, I didn't know until I overheard some of the others discussing the matter. It is a microchip that is implanted, quickly and simply by a syringe, just like a normal injection – it is only the size of a grain of rice, and as it's for a cat, it will be put just under the loose skin of the neck."

"You're kidding me."

"No, honestly Matt I'm not, Ben continued, "The microchip contains a fifteen digit code, so if you go missing and are found, most Vets, Rescue Centres and even local authorities have microchip readers which allow them to read the chip's code. This identifies the cat on a secure database, where all its details, such as breed, colouring, details of its age, name, size, description, home address and telephone/mobile numbers are registered."

I sat there amazed and thinking if only I had been microchipped by my owners they could have been traced, even though they had moved, by ringing their mobile number. Then I remembered they didn't own a mobile phone! Another thought then struck me, would I really have wanted to live again with the people who had so callously abandoned me. "No!"

"Is it really that simple?" I enquired.

"Yes, Matt is it. Also the database is accessible 24 hours a day 365 days a year, so you can be reunited with your owners again in no time at all, just by one telephone call" Ben concluded. "Oh, and the microchip is also invisible and cannot be tampered with, in case you are wondering."

"But what happens if owners move away," I enquired, curious now to want to know more.

"It's simple, your owners can use the online facility to easily update their contact details, Ben replied.

"It's a really cool method then," I stated remembering young Shaun's expression when I told him my name at my old home.

"Yes, Matt, even animals are surrounded by technology now."

"Well, thanks for all the information – it is really incredible, but you will say goodbye, before you leave," I pleaded.

"Of course Matt, but I haven't gone yet."

I padded back to my chosen spot at the back of the house and continued watching.

As soon as the first group of visitors had left the house, another group entered and thus I found myself watching the whole process again – children stroking the numerous cats and some of the adults doing the same, particularly those without any children in tow.

I also observed throughout the day, that each time a group left or entered the house, the gate to the main house was locked first, before the outer gate was unlocked and that that too, was locked immediately the last member of each group had left. There was definitely no escape.

So, it was, that a rather forlorn, though more informed cat, namely me, settled down resignedly at the end of my first day of experiencing visitors to the house – no one had even stroked me! My only consolation was that Ben was still here, along with Mitzi who had also been chosen, but that was a selfish thought, I just wished someone had chosen me.

Saturday 21st June and Sunday 22nd June

To-day and tomorrow, were also visitors' days, only being a weekend, a greater number of visitors arrived and departed. It fact it was quite mentally exhausting and consequently physically too. No, no one picked me or even picked me up, although a few people had remarked that they loved my colouring, in all five of us were chosen. Being totally honest, I breathed a sigh of relief when the last visitors left on the Sunday.

Monday 23rd June

A warm sunny day again, lots of cattering amongst the cats, otherwise nothing new to report.

Tuesday 24th June

Well, a lovely thunderstorm woke us all up after some long hot days. We all sheltered in the house and played "I spy" – yes, the children stole this game from the animal world – honestly! Though of course they didn't know this fact.

The staff had a lot of sweeping up to do as the outside area took a lot of the deluge.

Wednesday 25th June

To-day was to have been a visitors' day, but the car park was in a rather a bad state, we learnt from listening to Susan talking with one of the staff.

Mr. Harmer, the Vet visited and Ben was taken away briefly to be microchipped. Later Jason and his family returned to complete the necessary paper work and we all then sat and watched with envy as Ben was put into a pet carrier and removed from the house – bless him, he remembered to say goodbye to us all. We all knew we would never meet again.

Thursday 26th June

Mitzi left to-day, after being microchipped yesterday too, with a little girl, who beamed with happiness as much as Mitzi did – her parents looked delighted with their daughter's happiness too. Funnily enough, their happiness was infectious and even I and the others felt happy for them.

Friday 27th June to Friday 25th July

I spent the next four weeks, watching the visitors coming and going and each time I found the pain of rejection harder to bear, despite all Tom's previous reassurances. In fact Tom had himself had been chosen only three weeks after Ben and Mitzi left. Tom had of course made friends with many of the other cats and had also befriended quite a few of the new arrivals, besides myself, because he knew exactly how they felt, but despite all of this, nothing seemed to ease my pain and although I knew I was safe and being well cared for, I just wanted to feel special, wanted and loved by someone who I would in turn, also love. By the way I had another flea treatment on the 14th.

Also of course, I wanted to enjoy freedom again – to explore – to come and go as I pleased and freedom from the house, that had now become my cage.

Like all cats too, I just wanted to go out at night and hit the tiles! I hated having all my natural instincts suppressed, but worst of all was the knowledge that there was little I could do to change matters, unless I managed to escape by luck or guile. Continuously having my hopes raised and dashed, despite being complimented by numerous visitors that they loved my colouring, for some unknown reason still I wasn't chosen. Jill came in one day and took me into the shop with her for the day, even she had sensed my need for human company – we had quite a chat, with her sympathizing at my frustration and dismay.

Finally, she said, "Matt, if I take you home with me, just for a couple of nights, will you promise faithfully not to run away, because I would lose my job, if I did not return you to the Centre."

"Oh, Jill, I promise, promise, promise I will be a very good cat indeed – honestly – I always keep my word."

Saturday 26th July and Sunday 27th July

A fruitless weekend from my personal point of view, although a few more cats were chosen by happy children and parents, in fact even the newer cats were leaving and yet, I was still here.

Monday 28th July

Jill, true to her word, came to collect me at the end of the day, having earlier cleared everything with her boss. I was over the moon, I didn't even mind being put in a pet carrier, something which always gave me the collywobbles – made me nervous for the uninitiated. The other cats were not jealous; Mr. Tibbs and Lulubelle had told them how heartbroken I had become, so they were happy for me to have some respite from the house.

I was safely installed in the front passenger's well of Jill's car, like I had been in Vera's when she had first brought me to the Centre and off we went. Jill was kind enough to give me a running commentary of our journey. The countryside she described was full of tree lined lanes, with wild flowers gracefully flowering colourfully in the verges – we even passed a duck pond – I could hear them quacking!

"Here we are Matt, I only live twenty minutes from work and it is a lovely drive, apart from the cold icy days of winter. Now, I am going to take you inside with me and let you out into the garden for the evening. There is a stream at the bottom of the rear garden as well as dykes the other two sides, plus a locked gate in the fence that adjoins the cottage, otherwise the boss would not have allowed you to come home with me, however, you must keep to your promise as I'm not infallible."

"Jill, I have already promised not to escape, so please don't worry, I won't let you down ever." So saying I gave her one of my biggest smiles as she let me out of the pet carrier into the delights of her home.

I ran through the hall and into a truly delightful living room, full of chintzy curtains with matching furniture covers on the two armchairs and two seater settee. The carpet was a beautiful rust colour and my paws almost sank into it – I guess it was after the concrete floors of the pens and the house (cat house) that it felt so soft. I rolled over on the carpet in sheet delight – I was in a proper home at last – well, for a couple of nights – make the most of it Matt, I told myself.

I turned and watched Jill's face and the warmth that exuded from it as she grinned at my antics.

I'll show you the kitchen and give you some food, whilst I get myself a meal, then you can go and play in the garden for a while."

With my food eaten in minutes, I was at the back door of the kitchen calling for her to let me out.

"You will never tell anyone that I can talk to humans will you Jill, you see I only talk to people I instinctively feel I can trust."

"Course not Matt, now off you go and be good."

With a bound I was out of the door, across a small patio and on to the luscious looking lawn, which was mostly surrounded by a mix of busy lizzies, pansies and marigolds. It was stunning, especially after my long incarceration. I ran all the way to the end of the garden to look at the stream and amazingly spotted a heron standing absolutely still and upright. Despite being an extremely aware bird, I made him jump as I almost ran into him in my haste to see the stream.

"Sorry, Mr. Heron, didn't mean to startle you – you're quite safe from me – you're too big for starters," I quickly informed him.

"Look young man, I could give you a few really nasty pecks, if I was so inclined, so just think yourself lucky that I have had my fill of fish for the day."

I gulped, shut my mouth and gave him a smile, hoping that would resolve the matter.

"You were a bit too cocky, Matt," I scolded myself.

He gave me a disconcerting stare and then took off flapping his large deep grey wings. I watched in awe of his ability to fly until he disappeared from view, then returned my gaze to the stream.

I wondered if he had left any fish for me – yes, it was being greedy as I remembered I had already eaten. I spotted some sticklebacks finally; they were very difficult to see until they moved, "Don't worry you're too tiny for me" (not that they could hear me), I acknowledged as I peered into the depths for other signs of life.

I spotted the little black tadpoles, that would eventually grow into frogs and hop around Jill's lawn. Then I saw the ducks – mallards – mum and dad with their five chicks swimming to the side of the bank. Mum and dad spotted me at the same time and hissed at me as a warning, just in case I was considering attacking their brood. I wasn't, I was just fascinated by the wild life around me and soaking up my sense of freedom.

"It's okay Mr. and Mrs. Mallard, you and yours are quite safe – I was only admiring you and your family."

"We have to hiss or squawk at strangers, you see we are lucky if we manage to rear one chick, there are natural water predators that take them, such as otters."

"I understand, I'll leave you to enjoy your swim."

I left them swimming happily in the stream and strolled round to one of the dykes at the right side of the lawn. It was okay, but not so exciting as the stream, though I did see a pair of dragonflies hovering over the water and lots of midges flying around.

My curiosity satisfied for the moment, I strolled back towards the patio and the cottage. Jill had been watching me.

"I take it you enjoyed meeting all my friends that live at the bottom of the garden?" she asked.

"Yes, but I didn't see any fairies!"

She laughed at my joke and together we went indoors for the night. I slept incredibly well curled up on a beautiful soft rug in the kitchen – sheer bliss had descended.

Tuesday 29th July

"Wake up, sleepyhead, it's morning."

Jill's curtains in the kitchen were thick and so I hadn't been woken by the sun shining through them. I stirred myself slowly, as I took in again, but more thoroughly my new surroundings and sighed as I realised I wouldn't be here much longer.

"Matt, stop sighing, just enjoy the day and the time you are here – look upon it as a short holiday," Jill stated as she put my breakfast down in front of me.

She was right, I just had to make the most of to-day and the night, the future would take care of itself, as it always did; but for now, I was happy.

I apologized for my sigh and gratefully tucked into my morning feed as Jill sat at the kitchen table eating her breakfast, whilst reading her daily newspaper.

The excitement of the previous evening must have suddenly caught up with me, because I found myself feeling very tired. Noticing Jill was still reading her newspaper I padded over to my soft welcoming rug and curled up for a nap.

It was almost midday before I was woken by Jill stroking me.

"Gosh Matt, you must have been tired, you have slept almost the whole morning."

"It was all the excitement of last evening," I informed her. "What are we doing to-day?" I enquired.

"Well Matt, I have to go into the nearby broadland village and get some more supplies for myself and visit one of our charity outlets, that .raises money for St. Bernard's —we need as much money as possible, so we can carry on taking in rescue animals and feed them as well as paying the vet bills. I will be gone most of the afternoon, so I am sure you would rather play outside, wouldn't you?"

"Yes please Jill and I will behave myself too."

So Jill let me out into the garden along with a bowl of fresh water and locked up whilst I sat on the patio listening to her car driving off into the distance.

It was a glorious sunny summer's afternoon so I stayed on the patio for quite a while just breathing in the scent of the flowers and the fresh countryside air.

It was such a different experience from being locked in the house with the other cats at the Rescue Centre. I watched the branches of a nearby tree swaying in the light breeze; it felt as if it was the first time I had seen this, but of course if wasn't. My old home had a number of trees along the Avenue, I had taken them for granted that's all. I guess you have to truly lose things you love, before you fully appreciate their true worth.

"Gosh Matt, that was really philosophical," I told myself in amazement.

Then off I went once again to explore the garden. It was a lot larger than I had remembered from the previous evening. I decided to go slowly round each border, thus exploring every inch. I visited the large metal gate in the wall, finding of course that the bars were too close for even such a flexible cat like me to get through – no, I was not going to break my promise, just wanted to find out if I could escape!

Next, I went back down alongside the dyke, peering into its depths looking again for signs of life – there was plenty I know, but I think even the tadpoles were hiding underneath the water lilies. Then I saw Mr.Heron was back and ran bravely up to him. I sat as near as my courage would allow. Mr. Heron turned his long neck and looked down at me with his superior stare.

"I will say this for you young man, you are a brave cat, normally one stare is enough to frighten cats away for good, but you have come back for another – what are you doing here by the way, as I hadn't seen you before last evening?"

"Jill the owner of the cottage, has brought me here for a couple of nights as a break from the Rescue Centre," I answered.

"How did you end up at the Centre?"

"It's a long story and I don't want to bore you, basically I was abandoned, Mr. Heron – my name's Matt by the way."

"Rotten thing for your owners to have done – you can call me Mr. Heron."

"I do already." We both then laughed at this.

"Do you visit the stream every day," I enquired.

"No, but I do like the garden and I keep an eye out for Mr. and Mrs. Mallard and their latest brood of chicks – they should be along soon – they have a secret hiding place at night and so far the otter hasn't found it."

We chatted quite happily, though to any observer, we must have made a strange pair.

"If you will excuse the pun Matt, I must fly," Mr. Heron said laughing at his own joke and so off he flew.

I continued my ramble along the side of the stream, but didn't see Mr. and Mrs. Mallard or their chicks, so I continued along the other dyke until I ended up back on the patio. It was then I simply decided to just curl up and absorb the whole garden, so I would be able to keep the memory locked up inside me and if I ever felt downhearted again, I would remember last evening and this day with warmth and a smile.

I must have fallen asleep again, because the noise of Jill's car door slamming, woke me. I was at the kitchen door, almost before she entered the cottage – Jill was home.

"Hi Matt, have you enjoyed yourself to-day or did you just sleep?"

"Both – I met Mr. Heron again – he is an imposing enigmatic bird – we had a brief chat."

"Ah, so you animals can all talk to each other, I had often wondered if that was possible," came Jill's studied reply.

Yes, but you are unable to tell anyone – you promised before, now you must promise again."

"Matt, of course I will keep this secret too. I always keep my promises, unlike some people I could tell you about, but that's another story. Now what shall we get you for dinner?"

"Have you got any tuna – I quite like that " I replied.

"Actually I brought some whilst I was out, thinking you might like some as a treat."

I beamed!

Jill busied herself preparing my meal first and putting some fresh water in my bowl. I must admit I was a bit ravenous and ate it all very quickly, even Jill was amazed and gently scolded me for gulping my food down so quickly, telling me "it was not good for me, eating that quickly." Why do adults always think they know best?

I selfishly left Jill preparing her meal in the kitchen and wandered into the lounge, where I looked longingly at one of the lovely armchairs, should I crash out on one, or would Jill be annoyed? I decided to wait.

Jill came through eventually with her dinner and sat at the table; I waited expectantly by the armchair, hoping she would notice – she did!

"I take it you want to curl up on the armchair tonight Matt," she eventually stated.

"Please," replied I, doing an impersonation of a dog begging, by sitting on my backside and putting my front paws up in the curved down position.

"I'll get an old tea towel I keep just for cats and put it on the chair to protect it from your hairs."

It was duly brought and I was on the armchair in a flash – it was delightfully soft and I snuggled down for the evening."

"Are you going to watch any television or do you listen to the radio," I enquired, wondering what Jill was going to do after eating.

"As you are my guest Matt, you choose."

"What a thoughtful person Jill was," I thought. "I like all kinds of music Jill – there are only two kinds of music in all its forms, from pop, jazz, classical, big bands and country and western and that's good or bad. However, I wouldn't mind seeing the local news on the television first, if that's okay with you?"

"Goodness Matt, what a profound remark regarding music – you are quite right of course. It's half past six, so I'll put the local news on for us both."

I watched in silence as the local news was being shown – it seemed polite to do so.

I later informed Jill that I had got my love of music in all its forms from my previous owners and that I hoped any new owner would love music too.

"Ah, so it is still worrying you about being chosen – you will eventually Matt, everyone is, it is just a question of meeting the right prospective owner," she reassured me. We duly passed the rest of the evening listening to classical music on Classic FM

The sun was setting now and I looked at the golden/orange glow in the sky as it slowly set. It was a magical evening.

"You will have to go into the kitchen now for the night, it's an early start for us both in the morning, so we get to the Centre on time."

"Oh, Jill why did you have to remind me I was going back to the Centre tomorrow, I knew of course, but intended to think about it in the morning, not tonight, especially after a lovely day and evening" I said under my breath.

"Okay Jill, I'm off now to the kitchen, goodnight, sleep tight." I never mentioned my thoughts though.

Jill tidied up in the kitchen, so I settled down on the cosy rug – the morning would just have to take care of itself.

Wednesday 30th July

Jill's alarm clock woke me this morning – like all cats, my hearing was very acute. I guess it was back to the "salt mines" for Jill and the cat house for me.

I went into the pet carrier, like the good boy I was (well when I wanted to be!) and Jill put me into the car as before and off we both went to the Rescue Centre.

I got a lovely welcome from the other cats on my return, with all of them wanting to know what I had done and had I enjoyed myself. I was pleased and delighted too that no one expressed any jealousy.

By the end of the day, it had become a memory, but a good one.

Thursday 31st July to Monday 8th September

The weeks past and it was September now and I was horribly aware of the shortening days – a mixture of fear and panic went through me as I thought of the approaching winter and the possibility of spending it in the Cat house. I wanted to experience once again, the luxury and independence of living in my own home, but how and when? (14th August I had my monthly flea treatment and 22nd August my three monthly worming tablet.)

Tuesday 9th September

To-day turned out to be really heartbreaking for me; Mr. Tibbs and Lulubelle, with whom I had become great friends over the past two and a half months, left for a new home – a kind, attractive couple had chosen to take them both and they lived in a delightful country cottage, surrounded by fields in a nearby village. They said their farewells to everyone and I had to put on my bravest face as I watched them leave with their new owners. It wasn't sufficient though, for the tears had begun to run down my face as they disappeared out of sight, safely ensconced in separate pet carriers. I knew deep down that Mr. Tibbs and Lulubelle had struck gold for the couple who had taken them had fallen in love with Lulubelle immediately they saw her, but had not hesitated for one minute when they learnt that Mr. Tibbs had to be adopted too. In fact the lady had immediately made such a fuss of Mr. Tibbs, that I had almost felt the warmth flowing from her hand as she stroked Mr. Tibbs, myself.

Surely my turn had to come soon – it must!

WILLIAM, LAUREN & SAM

The ringing of the doorbell woke Lauren; she automatically looked at the clock; that's too early for the postman she thought, taking in the time – she was a night owl and was never at her best in the morning, neither was she dressed. She turned and gently shook William lying beside her.

"What is it?" William grunted.

"There is someone at the door, can you go I'm not dressed," Lauren answered.

The doorbell rang again – at this time in the morning – Lauren was now worried.

"Hang on I'm coming," William called out as he was halfway down the stairs.

William opened the door and there stood Jonathan.

"I think I've got Sam, he has been killed by a car I'm afraid."

Lauren heard every word, no! she almost screamed out. She leapt from the bed, slipped on her robe and ran down the stairs, to join William who had grabbed his dressing gown. Together they followed Jonathan across the road and along the path to his house, trying to convince themselves that it couldn't be Sam.

"It can't be Sam, he has a little metal disc attached to his collar with his name and telephone number on, Jonathan would have seen it," Lauren stated to William as she endeavoured to comfort herself and her husband.

They soon reached Jonathan's home, which was only about one hundred yards from their own door. They hurried together through Jonathan's gate and there on his patio was a small wicker basket containing a small body covered by a towel. Jonathan lifted the towel and there lay Sam.

The tears began to fall as Lauren reached down to stroke him, she just had to be certain he was really dead. Sam was cold to her touch, but she couldn't bring herself to stop stroking him, as if somehow that would bring him back to life.

"Come away; please leave him Lauren, there is nothing we can do," William pleaded as tears began to tumble down his cheeks too.

Lauren didn't want to leave Sam. She just wanted to carry on stoking him as long as possible so, even though she knew it was impossible, he could know just how much they loved him. Sam had been their friend and companion for over three years, since they first took him in as a stray when he had turned up at their back door, thin and miaowing pitifully.

William couldn't take it anymore and pleaded again for Lauren to leave Sam. Reluctantly she stood up and Jonathan's wife Diana gently wrapped her arms around Lauren, she and Jonathan were cat lovers too and knew how they were feeling.

"We will bury him in the garden." Lauren stated, "He loved it there."

But Jonathan intervened and said he knew of a Pet's Crematorium just a few miles away in the countryside, where he would take Sam for them. William and Lauren were grateful for his help as neither of them was emotionally capable of handling the situation.

"I'll bring the ashes back," Jonathan continued.

Lauren bent down and whispered a last goodbye to Sam – he had been so precious to them both. Clasping hands, William and Lauren walked back along the path and across the road to their home.

"We will get another one, won't we? William suddenly asked.

Lauren had had the same thought, but had felt it might upset William, if she expressed it.

"Yes," she almost wept in reply.

As they reached their door, she remembered it was Wednesday, that William had taken the day off work and that a ton of shingle was due to be delivered for Lauren to finish off landscaping their garden. It was also the 10th September and her husband's birthday. It was a day they had been looking forward to sharing with Sam, who had spent the last three months watching with curiosity as Lauren transformed the garden, lazing in the sun and just simply keeping her company. Now he would never see it finished. Lauren broke down once they were within the confines of their home and clung to William sobbing.

However, dealing with the shingle which arrived two hours later proved to be a distraction – it got them through the day.

Jonathan came round in the evening with a note of the telephone number of the Pet's Crematorium, where he had so kindly taken Sam for them.

"I'm sorry I couldn't bring Sam's ashes back with me, but all you have to do is ring and they will deliver the casket," he informed them.

Lauren rang the number and was informed that the casket would be delivered the next day. It duly was. They were originally going to bury him in the garden, but strangely enough the casket stayed on the shelf where Lauren had first put it and over the next few days both she and William knew that was where it would remain. They had a plaque engraved "SAM GREATLY LOVED" which was duly fixed to the casket.

It was now Sunday 14th September.

Lauren was grateful that William had agreed to have another cat. The love they had given so readily to Sam should not be allowed to die with him. They jointly decided that they would drive out to St.Bernard's

Rescue Centre, once the garden was finished and their emotions were not so raw. The Centre had been recommended to them by understanding friends.

It was fourteen days later, <u>Sunday 28th September</u>, that they made their way to Heighford, complete with a detailed map of how to reach St. Bernard's from this village. They had been told to turn right just before reaching the village pub, but after having first passed the village's church, also on their right.

Lauren was a careful driver and especially made a point of treating countryside roads with great respect, because round any blind bend there could be cyclists, a slow moving tractor, an idiot driver, ramblers, some of whom did not know that they should walk on the side of the road facing oncoming traffic when in the countryside, or the worse case scenario, a fallen tree. She also droved with dipped headlights in the daytime – she had learnt from her moped course many years earlier to always have her moped's headlights on so she could be seen easily and quicker; so when she now drove her car she adopted the same principle – she was also convinced that there would be less accidents if all car drivers followed suit, whatever the weather conditions. If anyone said anything, she always told them, the car thought it was a Volvo!

They both spotted the church on their right as they entered the village and Lauren duly remembered to turn right just before they reached the pub. William was always the navigator, a good one too, although he couldn't drive.

"Whereto next, William?" Lauren asked as she had now passed all her points of reference.

"Turn left," came the reply, but the direction came too late, Lauren had already passed the turn off, so she continued and finally found a turning space and turned the car round and drove back to the original turn off.

Turning left as originally instructed, she found she was driving even more carefully now as the taken country road became a narrow lane seeming to lead nowhere.

"This lane is almost a track now, William, are you sure we are on the right road?"

"Well there are no other roads marked, so we must be – just keep going."

Lauren drove on, but hoping that they didn't meet a car coming the opposite way – the last passing spot was now at least a quarter of a mile behind them. Suddenly she reached some crossroads.

"Which way William – straight on or do I take the right or left turning?"

"I should go straight on – the track looks rather narrow to the right and left."

Deep down, she felt they should have turned right, but Lauren continued on the same lane – it got narrower and narrower – Lauren became perturbed – there were no buildings in sight.

"This has got to be the wrong way William, I'm going to reverse back to the crossroads and take the right turning."

"You could be right, I must admit this lane seems a bit too narrow for any form of normal traffic."

Lauren slowly and painstakingly reversed back to the crossroads and turned right. She had only driven about three hundred yards when they both spotted the sign "St. Bernard's Rescue Centre." Lauren drove onto the gravelled forecourt in front of a large farmhouse and parked the car – they had arrived.

They made their way together towards the building marked Reception and entered hopefully.

"Hello," came the friendly voice of Jill as she welcomed the newcomers to the Centre. "How can I help you?"

Neither Lauren or William were shy people, so they came straight to the point.

"We're looking for a cat to give a loving home to."

DIARY OF MATT THE CAT

The next nineteen days passed slowly – nothing had changed in my life, apart from another monthly flea treatment on the 14th September.

Sunday 28th September

I was rudely waken from my afternoon nap in the sleeping quarters.

"Matt move yourself, there are some people coming to the pen."

I sleepily opened my eyes and looked up at the sound of Tiger's excited cry, he was one of the new intake.

"Not another group of visitors," I thought to myself. I turned on him.

"Tiger, I have had enough of hoping it might be my turn to find someone to love me again," I told him dejectedly. After all I had spent practically four and a half months in the main (pen) house, I had seen others come and go, but no one had shown even a flicker of interest in me, apart from Jill. I had even changed my attitude and approached most of the visitors and made myself agreeable, so why should to-day be any different. Tiger had become a new chum and I knew that it was because I had been so welcoming to him when he arrived, that he wanted to repay the kindness.

Tiger however, was determined and rushed back into the sleeping quarters to try and somehow drag me unwillingly and reluctantly into the main house.

Tiger pleaded, "Please Matt, don't give up, because if you do, you'll never succeed in leaving here, ever!"

Sometimes in life, you eventually realise, that there are some dreams you are not going to succeed in achieving, but in this particular case, I knew that Tiger was right. The trouble was I had had enough of being rejected time after time – Tiger had only been here a month – he couldn't possibly understand my despair.

I however, underestimated Tiger's determination to get me outside into the main area whether I felt like it or not, for Tiger gave me an almighty push with his head.

"If you do that again Tiger, I shall get very annoyed," I chastised him – "I'm tired, just let me sleep – if you like I'll come and play tag with you and the gang when everyone has gone home." I said this in the hope that Tiger would cease with his pushing. Instead he continued to plead.

"Oh Matt, I'm not bothered about a game of tag, I'd far rather see you happy – can't you face just half an hour outside?"

"Why should I Tiger," I responded wearily.

"Look, just to please me, compromise, so many things are worked out satisfactorily by this method, so come outside for half an hour and I promise to leave you alone if you do," Tiger continued. Tiger's remark stunned me – he was wise for a youngster, so I looked up at his eager face and found my resolve softening.

"Okay, I'll come outside for half an hour and then I am going back to sleep," I responded as emphatically as I could.

"Good – well out you go then," so saying Tiger gave me yet another shove, only more forcibly this time. I was seriously tempted to give Tiger a rebuking smack with my paw, but knowing it would be a petty gesture, wisely decided against it. Once outside in the fresh September air, I found I was glad at first just to walk around in the open. I even found myself eyeing the approaching visitors.

"Just the usual bunch," I thought cynically.

I pulled myself up short, I didn't whatever happened to me, want to become a cynic putting everything and everyone down – I had been an optimist before my abandonment. So, I watched casually as the group entered the house and began slowly mingling themselves amongst the numerous cats who were already gathered there. I noticed a lady staring at me and was puzzled, but decided I might as well wander over, so I jumped up onto a ledge which ran the length of the pen and moved in closer towards her. To my surprise, she stroked me and I found myself rubbing my head against her hand time and time again. Jill for once, had accompanied the visitors into the pen and noticed the contact between us. I heard Jill call out "Lauren, his name is Matt, he was found abandoned in a house, apparently the owners just moved out and left him there."

"What a heartless thing to do," I heard Lauren answer.

So, Lauren was kind I surmised. I decided to stay a little longer, still allowing myself to be stroked. It became an enjoyable moment, but my fear of being rejected yet again, got the better of me and I suddenly decided to move away. I turned and walked back along the ledge and leapt onto one of the tables and began to wash myself nonchalantly, yet my curiosity got the better of me. I cautiously eyed the lady again and noticed that she had been joined by a male companion – then that they were talking. I had, to my annoyance, moved myself too far away to hear their discussion. I noticed the lady, I remembered Jill had called Lauren, looking at me again, but the next moment she and her companion left the house.

"Another rejection, why did I bother," I muttered angrily to myself. "I just wish I could leave this house as easily as the visitors." I still wanted so much to be free again to roam at will. Tiger, who had been watching had sensed my mood and feeling guilty for persuading me to forego my sleep padded over to me to apologise.

"It's okay Tiger, your intentions were good, but please don't disturb me again when we have visitors," I generously replied. I really had had enough of false hopes. The next four days passed uneventfully.

Friday 3rd October

Tiger and I were sitting outside the sleeping quarters, in the autumn sunshine and were idly watching as Angela approached the house carrying a large pink plastic carrier.

"Someone's going to a new home Matt, I wonder who it is?" Tiger piped up.

"Well, it's not going to be me, I can tell you that now," I snapped back at him. I truly had had enough of false hopes and besides, the pet carrier was pink – a female's colour. However, I was curious to see who was going this time and watched Angela intently.

I selfishly hoped it wasn't Tiger; he had become a good mate, despite his over enthusiasm at times. Angela entered the house and walked over to me, putting the pet carrier down besides me and opening its grilled front gate.

"Come on Matt – it's finally your turn to leave us – your new owners are waiting in the main office, so in you go."

Before I had time to take in her words, I was popped into the carrier, the grilled front gate shut and I was on my way. I peered out and managed to wave goodbye to Tiger by pressing my front paws against the grill. Tiger returned my wave with a large smile on his face.

Angela had to put the pet carrier down to unlock the cat house and when outside she put me down again, whilst she locked up – meticulous as ever. Tiger bounded over.

"Be happy Matt, you deserve it – you've been such a good friend to me," he managed to whisper before Angela whisked me away from the house, then through the outer gate, unlocking and locking it behind her. Now we were travelling across the gravelled forecourt.

Angela hurried into the main office with me, where I saw a lady and her companion busy reading and filling in adoption forms. Angela put the carrier with me still inside onto the larger counter.

"There you are Matt – you can see what is going on from up here. I'll say goodbye now, it has been a pleasure to have you here, but I know you must be thrilled to be leaving at last." With those parting words she hurried away to attend to the other animals in her care. She had, I know grown fond of me soon after I first arrived, but like most of the staff, preferred not to show any preference towards the animals in her care, but would do so, if none of the other animals were around.

I peered through the grill and noticed that it was the same lady and gentleman who had visited the house five days earlier – then I recognized her – it was Lauren, who I had let stroke me for a while, before I had turned on my heels and watched from a distance.

"Was I really, really, going to a new home and to be loved by someone again," I wondered.

My little heart began to beat faster with excitement at the thought – was I actually going to be free again to roam, explore, to come and go as I pleased. I must be, for surely no one would put me in a pet carrier if I wasn't leaving.

I noticed that Lauren was reading the forms along with her companion.

"Hurry up and sign them – I want to go now – I've been here four and a half months – I want my freedom," I wanted to shout at them both. "If they could only read my thoughts," I sighed. "Patience Matt," I muttered under my breath.

Unfortunately for me, Lauren always read any forms through thoroughly that she had to sign – she had apparently, I learnt later, once been a legal secretary and therefore followed the invaluable advice of always, but always, read any forms through before signing them.

"William, what do you think about this paragraph," Lauren asked.

"Ah, so your name is William, that's cleared that point up for me."

I listened as Lauren and William then queried a couple of points on the form and finally, being satisfied as to their meaning, duly signed the Adoptions Forms.

Then Jill spoke.

"You will need these; they are Matt's medical records relating to vaccinations and the other form details his name, age, sex, he has been neutered of course, breed, colouring and when his next flea drops, worming and vaccination are due, along with his known history and full details of how to look after him when you get him home. He has also been microchipped by the way. We do that to all the animals. All Matt's details are already registered and we will now inform the firm holding them of your names, address and telephone and mobile numbers, so their records can be updated."

"It's fascinating what they do now – we had a lovely cat called Sam and we chose Matt because he was the only one who appealed to us – his colouring reminded us of Sam, so we know how to look after him," explained Lauren and William almost in unison.

"Yes, I know," replied Jill. "Unfortunately, we have to follow the rules to make certain each animal will be looked after properly when they leave here."

"That's the trouble with life to-day, too many rules!" responded William, though good humouredly.

I listened flabbergasted at all the detailed information that Lauren and William had to have about me, before I could leave. It had seemed so simple at my old home.

"I'm glad he has been microchipped, it makes life so much simpler if he goes missing and is then found," Lauren stated.

"Yes," I thought, "I can always be traced now."

"I see he mustn't be allowed out for at least two to three weeks, but surely he can have some fresh air during that time," Lauren enquired, remembering the form's contents, which she wanted to double check.

"Two to three weeks before I'm allowed out – you must be joking," I muttered angrily. "We'll see about that – I've already been locked up for months."

Now I was really angry.

"Yes, but he has to get use to his new surroundings and know that the place is his home and where to find his food," had come Jill's reply.

"It also says here, that when you first let the cat out of the house, you must go with it and stay with it – how do we do that without him dashing off," William interjected.

"You can put him on a lead just like you would a dog and gradually the trips outside can become longer," I heard Jill respond. "We have some leads on the shelf behind you."

"Lead – no one is going to put me on a lead, I'm not a dog," I wanted to scream out. I was really, really getting seriously annoyed now.

"Abandoned, taken to a Rescue Centre, then almost five months later, someone is being told to treat me like a dog and without any freedom for another two to three weeks!" My fighting spirit had returned at last – no one, but no one, is putting me on a lead." I stamped my paw angrily on the clean paper lining the pet carrier, but no one, unfortunately heard me.

"Have you got flea drops for him?" Jill enquired of my new owners.

"Yes, we've still got three months supply we had for Sam," Lauren answered. "I note from the forms that you can visit the adopted animals to inspect it and the conditions it is being kept in, without notice, at any reasonable time," Lauren continued with her queries.

"That's correct," Jill replied. "You see, although we have already checked out who you are and where you live, we are obligated to check on the animal. I'm sure you can appreciate that."

I continued listening intently, though I did wonder if Jill had temporarily forgotten I could understand every word. It was a pity I couldn't risk having a brief chat!

"Of course we do," William stated and wanting to get going he asked, "To whom do I make out the cheque in respect of Matt's adoption fee?"

"St.Bernard's Rescue Centre, please and thank you once again for adopting one of our animals – I would be grateful too, if at anytime you have family or friends wishing to adopt, you would recommend us to them."

"We most certainly will, won't we Lauren."

Lauren readily agreed. I watched as William filled in the cheque, signed it and handed it over with the rest of the forms, duly signed, now that he was satisfied that their queries had been answered.

"Come on young man, it's time we got you home – goodbye and thanks," came William's departing words.

At last – I had never known about the actual adoption procedure before or that it was so thorough and took so long – although I was delighted to be going, I was pleased when Jill's face peered at me through the grilled gate.

"Goodbye Matt, I shall miss you," she whispered.

"Goodbye Jill, I'll miss you too," I managed to whisper back before I was whisked away by William. I never had the chance to thank her.

William got into the back of the car and placed the pet carrier with me inside, beside him before belting up.

I noticed however, that he kept his hand firmly on the carrier.

Lauren duly got into the driver's seat, belted up too and we were on our way.

I couldn't see much from where I was, all I could do was peer up at William and study his face. It was rounded, but with a strong jaw line and when he looked at me and smiled, not only did his handsome face light up, but his beautiful blue eyes sparkled with life. I then wondered what Lauren looked like close to, as I hadn't really fully studied either of them when they came to the house.

I managed to make out the tops of trees as we drove down the lane towards the main road in the village. I could just see glimpses of the sky too. How long would the journey take, what would my new home be like; there were so many thoughts and questions now buzzing around in my mind. I hoped however, it was a friendly neighbourhood, like my last abode. Would there be any other cats living nearby. I might have hated being in the cat house for all those long months, but I had always had company there, though I had to confess I had deeply missed being loved and cuddled. I so hoped Lauren and William would truly love and care for me. I hoped too that I would get to love Lauren and William. Being really truthful, I never wanted to be shut up in a pen again – ever!

It seemed to be a long journey, but eventually William, who had kept a keen watch on me, spoke.

"Not far now, young man."

Lauren duly turned left and drove into a Close and parked in the drive of their home, soon to be mine too – the car could be put away later.

Suddenly, I became fearful as William opened the car door. Where exactly was I, would I like my new home? The pet carrier swayed as William lifted it off the back seat and I found myself letting out a nervous cry.

"It's okay Matt you're home," William reassured me.

"Home, what a beautiful word," I thought.

Now, after my initial nervousness, I began to get excited.

"What would their home be like, would it have a garden, where would I sleep and gosh I'm hungry too," I found myself muttering to myself.

We entered through the front door, into a spacious hall and thence into the kitchen.

"Wow!" I said to myself – this is huge," as William put the pet carrier down.

"Come on, come, open the gate, I want to explore and I want some food too," I squeaked – well almost.

I heard the rattle of a box of crunchies – it was music to my ears – I was now really eager to get out of the carrier somehow.

"At last, it's about time you let me out," I grumbled as William lent down and opened the grilled gate.

In a flash, I was out – where was the bowl with the crunchies – then I saw the bowl full of lovely different shaped crunchies – I wondered what the flavour was.

"Eat them you idiot, then you will find out," I chastised myself.

I tucked in, the crunchies were salmon, tuna and shrimp flavoured and they were absolutely delicious! Next moment the other part of the bowl was filled - I glanced at it – chicken – not tinned, real chicken meat!

"Crickey, more food, they must think I'm starving. Best not to gorge too much, or I'll make myself sick," the thought almost made me stop eating. "I did say almost!"

Hunger satisfied, a water bowl appeared – I drank eagerly.

Suddenly I found myself being lifted up and carried across a hall and into the living room, where I was placed onto a dumpy – a low padded seat, footstool, whatever, in case you are wondering, what's a dumpy.

Then I felt my old collar being removed and in its place a bright fluorescent yellow collar was fastened. I liked it. I noticed it had a small disc with my name and a telephone number engraved upon it. It also had attached a small bell. I shook my head – it rang, so I shook my head again.

"That's so we can hear you coming Matt and the disc will inform people of your name and how to contact us, should you get lost in your new surroundings," I heard Lauren informing me.

I looked up, tilted my head to one side and studied her face. Her skin was tanned from the summer that had passed, her warm auburn hair encroached upon her cheeks and just touched her shoulders. She smiled at me and just like William's smile, her face lit up and her dark brown eyes sparkled behind a pair of attractive half rimmed lilac spectacles. I noticed too her very firm jaw line.

"Your litter tray is in the kitchen for the night and we will take you for a walk tomorrow and show you the garden."

"A garden," I sighed with relief, the house had a garden where I could play. Nobody should live in a house without a garden, it's essential for your health to have somewhere to relax and unwind, especially on a summer's day. Besides, it's also a place to glory in the growth of beautiful flowers and shrubs and watch the bees gathering the pollen. I sighed again, even though it was autumn.

"Hang on there Matt, Lauren said tomorrow, what's wrong with to-day. I know it will soon be dark outside, but I would really like to stretch my legs."

Then I remembered they had been told to put me on a lead like a dog! I listened from the dumpy as Lauren and William tidied up in the kitchen. I had noticed it was modern with all the appliances fitted, except for a large pine dresser.

"Good, I can hide behind that – I must have a cubby hole," I thought.

I had also noticed a small cat bed in the corner beside the dresser – mine! I yawned – I was tired – it was all the excitement, for it had been a day to remember. I had left the Rescue Centre, was finally in a new home with two people who wanted me; I had been well fed and watered and now I suddenly realised I just really wanted to sleep – the strain of the past months had left their mark. I heard William and Lauren come into the living room.

"Come on William, Matt's tired, let's go to bed now – it's been a strange day, but I'm glad we have one of "the little people" with us again."

68

I waited, William agreed, for he was tired too. I was gently gathered up and returned to the kitchen and my bed. They both pattered and stroked me gently. I purred with pleasure and smiled to myself – I even felt happy. I also liked being called "one of the little people" – what a lovely phrase.

Lauren switched off the kitchen light, gave me a final stroke as I settled down into my basket, said goodnight and shut the door behind her. I heard them cross the hall and begin to climb the stairs to where I assumed was their bedroom.

I decided I would have to explore the rest of the house tomorrow and there was the walk to look forward to, even if it was on a lead!

I settled myself down for the night in the lovely square brown leather cat bed with a cream coloured fleece inside it, covered with a fresh small towel to protect the fleece. I would sleep well tonight. Upstairs Lauren and Willim would sleep well too.

Saturday 4th October.

I heard Lauren and William coming down the stairs, they had woken early. I quickly stood up, arching my back and then relaxing, stepped out of my lovely warm bed, then stretched out my front legs, followed by my rear ones. Morning exercises finished, I padded over to the dumpy which had been moved from the living room to the kitchen and sat on it, facing the door expectantly, for to-day I was going to go for a walk OUTSIDE!

"Hello Matt," Lauren and William greeted me in unison.

I waited for what was going to happen next.

"William will give you a comb through, whilst I get our breakfasts and yours," Lauren informed me.

I was pleased that they both talked to me – perhaps as I got to know them better, I would surprise them and reply. I don't like being combed though, as you already know and William was about to find this out as he walked towards me with a steel cat comb.

Bending down towards me he began firmly combing my back. To my surprise I did nothing, whereas I had prepared myself ready to turn on him and scratch.

"On your side next young man," and with those words I found myself being bodily lifted and laid on my side. William then preceded to comb my right side and then my left side, but still I did nothing untoward.

"Over you go," William instructed as he rolled me on to my back.

"Oh no I don't," I muttered as I found myself lunging at William with my claws.

"I do not like my tummy being combed, thank you very much, as you are now finding out."

"Ouch, Matt that hurt," William cried out. "Lauren I think we have a cat with a mean streak here."

"No, I wasn't mean – I just didn't like my tummy being combed!".

Lauren came over immediately.

"You're not mean are you Matt," she said, more as a statement of fact, than as a question. "You must have pulled some of his hairs."

She was blaming William!

"Well you come and comb him then and see how he treats you," William responded.

Lauren took the comb from William's outstretched hand and preceded to comb me. My sense of humour wickedly took over and I deliberately decided to bide my time with Lauren and behave – besides it would make William wonder why he had been scratched and Lauren hadn't. It was my way of having fun with both of them. I watched William's surprised face and smiled to myself. After Lauren had finished I padded over to my feeding bowls and sat beside them expectantly. They duly took note and laughed, before filling them with food, crunchies and water.

"See you later, Matt," they both stated, before shutting me in the kitchen, as they took their breakfast cereals and morning tea back up to bed with them, together with a few pages from the morning's paper, which had been delivered, whilst I was being combed.

"Hey," I wanted to call after them, "What about my walk?"

The door stayed shut behind them.

It was almost an hour later that William opened the door to the kitchen again, so I shot out and ran into the hall towards the front door, but William didn't follow, so I returned to the kitchen and made for the back door.

"I suppose you would like a breath of fresh air," enquired William, at last cottoning on to what I was up to.

"Too true I would, so when can I be let out please?" I muttered hopefully to myself.

"Lauren, I'm going to take Matt for a quick walk around the garden, do you want to come?" I heard William call out – he didn't need to go to the foot of the stairs – Lauren's hearing was very acute.

"Yes, hang on, I'm coming down," I heard Lauren reply.

I sat impatiently waiting and thinking. A walk was really the last thing on my mind, I wanted some real freedom, so I could roam again and I was determined that it would be to-day, but first I would have to let them take me out into the garden.

William held me firmly in order to allow Lauren to clip the lead onto my collar.

"Great, now I feel like a dog!" I was getting annoyed now. "Thank goodness my mates at the Rescue Centre can't see what I have been reduced to," I growled under my breath.

William opened the back door.

"Come on young man, just a gently walk around the garden, so you can get some fresh air and we'll also show you your living quarters, so you will be able to come and go as you please when we are out, after your two week confinement in the house." William informed me as he gently lifted me up and deposited me on the path outside the kitchen door.

"Living quarters?" I was puzzled now, for I had assumed that the house was to be my residence. However, deciding it was prudent to go for a

71

walk first, before attempting to escape from the confines of the lead, I dutifully padded beside William and Lauren, along the garden path outside their kitchen window at the same time giving their garden the once over.

I noted their beautifully manicured lawn, together with the neatly laid out flower beds. I padded past their metal garden gate, noting the driveway on the other side, but also noting the gate was padlocked and that the bars were too close together for me to squeeze through. Turning right, I was now strolling along the path besides their large garage, dividing them from their neighbours. Upon reaching the end of the garage, we turned right again, crossing the back of the lawn beyond which was a large shrubbery area in front of their rear wall. Next, we passed their patio area complete with table and chairs and turning right again followed another path that ran along another high side wall, which I assumed belonged to their other neighbours' garage.

"Believe you me, I felt really undignified and stupid being led on a lead."

"Here's your living quarters," stated William as we stopped outside a small shed, close to their kitchen door. It seemed my tour was complete.

Having taken a thorough note of all my surroundings, I decided that it was time to attempt to make my escape from the lead. My pride, remember was at stake here.

I stopped suddenly; I had already felt that the collar was rather loose around my neck as the walk had commenced. I gave one quick backward pull. I had been right, the collar was loose enough – I was FREE!

Turning swiftly I ran towards the waterbutt I had noticed beside the shed – I leapt onto it, another leap found me on top of the shed and yet another leap took me on to their neighbours' wall.

Then I head the panic in William and Lauren's voices as they called out to me to come back, but I was off, free to explore. I took a deep breath – even their air felt fresher to my nostrils. I reached the end of the wall and half slid/walked down it onto a wide pavement.

"Made it!" I let out a triumphant cry of excitement and relief as I safely landed. Giving a quick backward glance, I realised I was out of William and Lauren's sight.

"Matt! Come back please," I heard Lauren pleading. "William what are we going to do, he's not suppose to be out on his own for at least two weeks; the Rescue Centre will say we've been negligent.

"Don't panic Lauren; we'll catch him – he won't go far – remember this area is totally unfamiliar to him," I heard William state, endeavouring to console Lauren. He had realised it was no good both of them panicking.

I decided to briefly stay within earshot, so I could hear what they were deciding to do.

"If you stay here, just in case he decides to return and I go to the end of the Close and then double back checking in each garden, as I cannot see him crossing the main road, I should be able to find him," I heard William inform Lauren – I knew he was kidding her, for I couldn't remember when I had felt so exhilarated. After all these months I was at liberty to run with the wind, to chase birds, well it's what we cats do, to explore and perhaps make new friends, but best of all, I no longer had any boundaries to my life.

Knowing that William was coming after me, I didn't want to waste any time in setting off to explore the immediate area and where it might take me.

It didn't matter where the pavement led, but I knew that to fully enjoy my freedom, I would have to move quickly. I ran along the pavement, gathering speed as I passed their neighbour's front garden, then the next house, until I finally reached the end of the Close.

At the end of the Close, I found a road – a busy one too. However, I was very street wise and waited until it was absolutely safe to cross. I did this by looking right, then left, then right again and seeing the road was clear both ways trotted across, still checking the road. Once I found myself on the opposite pavement, I took in the row of neat bungalows, but I had spotted lots of trees behind them.

"Come on Matt make your mind up, you are a sitting cat if you don't get a move on." I had to decide quickly – I really didn't have any time to waste, William could still find me.

It was then I noticed someone walk out of a pathway about fifty metres away.

"A way in to the trees and beyond, let's go Matt." Thus motivated I made a dash for the pathway. "Where would it lead?"

On reaching the end of the pathway, I was stunned.

"Wow," I breathed in delight – I couldn't believe it – I was in the countryside.

Ahead was a forest of trees, with a myriad of paths. I wasn't to know that I was on the outskirts of the town in an area where houses could not be built – to me it was heaven – somewhere to roam and frolic in the longish grass and climb the beckoning trees. I made for the nearest one and climbed it with such enthusiasm that I was well over halfway up within seconds and padding along a large branch.

"You can slow down now," I told myself. "No one is going to find you up here."

So I paused and took in my new surroundings, enjoying the wonderful sense of freedom that was overwhelming me. It had been far too long in coming, so I was enjoying myself, just savouring every precious • moment whilst I could.

I stretched out along the branch hiding behind its leaves; I let out a deep sigh of satisfaction and smiled to myself, delighting in the sheer pleasure of having climbed a tree again. I loved the smell of the leaves, which were still in abundance, despite the autumnal nip in the air.

Then I heard William and also Lauren calling my name. At first I froze, then relaxed spreading my lithe body flat against the branch. I had waited months for this feeling of release and dare I say it, happiness – it was mine to enjoy, it was deserved, for how often had I peered through the fence of the pen at the Rescue Centre, sometimes weeping, promising myself that one day I would be free. Yes, it was selfish, but only in relation to William and Lauren, who I hoped would understand.

I peered down the path wandering whether William and Lauren would take it and watched with delight mixed with a tinge of guilt, when they turned back retracing their steps, but obviously still searching for me.

"So they didn't think I would have come this far," I thought to myself. "Little do they know me then." Yet I was surprised and hated my arrogance.

I also realised the stupidity of this thought – for let's face it, William and Lauren barely knew me – come to that, I didn't know them either, though I realised that their anxious searching for me meant that they cared about me and wasn't that what I wanted. Of course it was, but for now I was not going to give up my new found freedom. Though to be honest I did feel some shame at my behaviour.

I was startled as I heard a movement above me and looked up, only to see a small grey squirrel with a very long bushy tail, peering down at me. We eyed each other tentively though each of us knew instinctively we were safe. I would have liked to play, but I still just wanted to take in more of my new surroundings, before attempting more exploration.

"I'm new here," I stated by way of explanation.

"Yes, I know," replied the squirrel, "All the squirrels here know the regular cats, that's why I've come down to check you out – I'm Nutty, by the way."

"Pleased to meet you, Nutty – I think your name's crackers!" "Sorry, I just like making jokes. I suppose you are called that for obvious reasons," I enquired. "My name's Matt."

"Afraid so, I'm not daft you know, it's just because I'm nearly always eating them, apart from when I'm storing up nuts and other food for the winter months. Do you want to come and meet some of the others?"

I deliberated, perhaps it would be better to meet some new friends, whilst I had the opportunity – I could still do some more exploring later.

"I'd love to, whereabouts are you living?" I enquired.

"It's not far, we have a lovely hideaway, where no one can ever find us – just follow me."

Nutty then scampered, along his branch and started down the trunk of the tree, his long furry tail, bobbing behind him. I followed Nutty, marvelling at the dexterity and speed of my new found friend, who had already reached the bottom of the tree, whilst I had only covered half the distance.

"Come on slowcoach," Nutty laughingly called out.

"It's okay for you, you are not only lighter and smaller bodied than me, but you also have a very long bushy tail to help you keep your balance, so be patient with me please," I retorted.

"Don't fret, I was only teasing," came the reply.

"Yes, I know you were, so I am not annoyed."

Nutty then bounded away with me running after him – to an onlooker it would have seemed that a cat was chasing a squirrel, instead of following one!

I wondered expectantly, where this little adventure would lead. Then Nutty bounded off towards some very long grass about twenty metres away.

 Suddenly, as I had almost caught him up, Nutty disappeared beneath some large bushes. I stopped puzzled, where could he be? The next moment he popped up again, just inches from me.

"Come on in."

I paused, a bit wary now, then pushed my body cautiously through the bushes, until I found myself at the entrance to Nutty's hideaway. I hesitated again, I wanted to meet Nutty's friends, but felt decidedly nervous at entering what appeared to be a burrow.

"How far down do we have to go?" I enquired. To be honest I was bothered that once down the burrow I might not be able to turn around, worse, I might get stuck.

"You're fretting again, Matt. It's a very large burrow, especially after you have managed the first few metres."

Having plucked up the courage, to my amazement, I found myself going underground along a tunnel, which then diverged into numerous passages – it was incredible. I also found I could see, as the tunnels and passageways were lit by fireflies, a nocturnal beetle, who were giving off a greenish glow (the wingless females and larvae of which are known as glowworms).

"Excuse me, Nutty," I called out. "What are the fireflies doing down here, they normally live in the tropics or warmer regions than here?" I asked fascinated.

"You are quite correct Matt, we found them living here after the rabbits vacated the burrows, we are now travelling along – the general consensus is that they escaped from a butterfly farm or something similar and then evolved to our climate; they are quite happy down here living with us, when we are hiding away, especially of course in the winter, though we do not hibernate you know, although there is a larger breed of squirrel than us tree dwelling ones, that are true ground dwellers, who do live in burrows and even may hibernate for many months." Nutty continued to feed me more information.

"Do you know Nutty, I always thought you squirrels hibernated, because you stored food for the winter. I am amazed at what I am learning."

"Ah, just because we store food, doesn't mean we hibernate, it's just because our type of food isn't around in the winter." Then Nutty was off running again.

Feeling much happier and encouraged by what I was seeing and the fact that the tunnel was wider than I had originally thought, I continued to follow Nutty.

Then we entered a large chamber and there were Nutty's friends.

Six pairs of studious eyes greeted me as I padded into the chamber watching my every move, as I duly stretched my hind legs and then my front legs, before sitting down. This truly was an adventure.

Nutty began to introduce me to the six squirrels, who immediately began to chatter excitedly amongst themselves, before politely offering me some liquid refreshment – I was amazed that they had a supply of water in the chamber, though I also noticed the large store of nuts and berries in a very large cubby hole set in one of the walls.

Then I caught Nutty watching my expression as well as following my gaze.

"We're a lot more cleverer than people think, Matt. We found an underground spring in the forest and we go regularly and collect a supply, so it's quite fresh for you to drink."

I drank the water gratefully, I had had such an adventurous day that it was only now that I realised how thirsty I actually was.

"Are you hungry?" asked one of Nutty's friends, "Though I'm afraid we've only got nuts and berries."

"Thanks for the water, Nutty, but I think I'll forego your friend's offer of nuts and berries, if you don't mind. Do you sleep down here?" I asked out of curiosity.

The squirrels all twittered lightheartedly at the question, before replying almost in unison.

"Only when it's really cold or very wet outside, we're tree squirrels you see and prefer to be outdoors as much as possible, though you have to be sharp eyed to spot us in the trees. We store the food down here for the winter and to keep it dry."

I smiled at their enthusiasm in imparting this knowledge to me. I had met some squirrels in the past, but had never got into any form of conversation with them.

"Well, I have learnt a lot to-day," I responded.

"I bet that we can tell you something else about us that you didn't know," Nutty spoke up teasingly.

"Go on then, surprise me," I replied encouragingly.

"Well, you will be surprised, because not many people know our young offspring are called kittens at birth, like yours," finished Nutty chuckling as he watched my surprised expression.

"You're joking aren't you," I replied somewhat staggered.

"No, I'm absolutely serious – so there you are – we have something in common that you would never ever have suspected," Nutty continued delightedly, as all the other squirrels giggled.

I began to giggle too, as it seemed such an incredible fact, so incredible that I wanted to tell all the cats I knew – it was then I remembered I had only been in this neighbourhood for a day and didn't have any friends I could tell. This thought brought on the sadness of my abandonment again. Next I remembered that I had deserted William and Lauren who were offering me a new home – I was struck with guilt.

"What's the matter Matt?" said Nutty noticing my pained expression, yet giggling at the words matter Matt!

"I'm sorry Nutty, it's just that I've been through a few traumatic months and the pain keeps coming back – it just sweeps over me – worse I have just deserted my new owners. You won't be offended will you, if I just go off on my own and catch up with you all again some other time, I have so enjoyed your company."

I waited for their response.

"Oh Matt, I'm so sorry, look I'll take you back through the burrows and any time you want to talk, just drop in, there's generally someone here, especially now as the nights are drawing in," Nutty replied for them all and began to lead me back along the burrows and into the open air, but not before I had said a fond farewell to my new friends.

Taking a deep breath of fresh air, as we reached the hidden entrance, I shook Nutty's front paw and patted him gently with my paw in appreciation of his kindness and friendship. I knew I had found a friend. Nutty unbeknown to me, watched me depart until I was out of sight.

I, of course, was now downhearted and back to reality. I was also ashamed. I knew that I ought to return to William and Lauren, but the pull of being free to roam after the past few months was stronger; thus I set off once again to explore my new environment. It was late afternoon, before the events of the day caught up with me – I had just climbed onto the roof of a small shed, when tiredness hit me so hard, that after one large yawn and having curled myself into a small ball of fur I fell asleep.

Sunday 5th October

I was woken from my slumbers to-day by the sound of the birds chirping nearby. In fact my ears pricked up the moment I heard the sound – birds were always a challenge to cats! (Sorry bird lovers!)

I sat bolt upright listening intently, I could hear them, but they were certainly not within striking distance, in fact to my annoyance I couldn't even see them.

The sun was up too and I felt its welcoming warmth flood through me as I stirred myself.

It was then, I remembered yesterday and the adventures, plus the shame of being truly naughty.

"It's about time I went home, though I am sure to be severely and deservedly chastised," I muttered away.

I was surprised to realise that I was already thinking of William and Lauren's abode as home, especially as I had only spent one night there. Therefore somewhat puzzled, I went through my waking up stretches, before setting off for 'home.'

I leapt from the roof of the shed and onto a lower wall before half sliding down onto the pavement of the road, which I remembered from the previous day, I was lucky. I had slept on a shed roof right close to the road I had crossed the previous day. From here it was a piece of cake to find my way back to William's and Lauren's. I crossed the road just as carefully as I had done yesterday.

"Why people believe cats need to get use to their new environment gradually, I was at a loss to understand," I chatted to myself as I scampered along the pavement of the Close towards 'home.'

I reached the neighbour's house and leapt onto their wall padding along till I reached William's and Lauren's shed, which I remembered was to be my living quarters. I leapt onto it's roof. Having reached this far, I began to wonder what kind of reception I would receive on my return. I padded round to the other side of the shed looking for the water butt.

"There he is!" Lauren's cry of relief reached William's ears and mine at exactly the same time. I felt really guilty now.

"Well at least I'm not in their black book then," I thought as I leapt down onto the water butt, then slid down onto the path where I found myself being swept up into William's arms.

"Come on young man, it's indoors for you from now on," I was informed as I was firmly deposited onto the dumpy in the kitchen, much to my annoyance.

"No, I wanted to scream out, not indoors again – can't you see that I've come back of my own free will, that I do want to live here; come on play fair," but my unspoken thoughts of course went unheard.

I asked myself, "Should I behave or try for another escape?"

"Hang on, you idiot, you haven't eaten since yesterday; best behave then," I wisely told myself.

I watched William and Lauren carefully, wandering what they really thought, then William spoke again.

"We will have to make certain he stays in for the next two weeks Lauren. I know we are both relieved to see Matt again, but if we had lost him, even though it was really Matt's determination to escape, we would have been held responsible and in breach of our contract with the Rescue Centre."

I waited expectantly for Lauren's reply – would she agree with William? She came over and took me from William's arms and held me firmly in hers.

"Look Matt, we both understand your desire for freedom, but you must be patient – now I'm, going to comb you, whilst William will get your breakfast," so saying Lauren went and got what was to become my comb and began grooming me.

"Here we go again," I muttered to myself, "I don't mind my back, sides or chin being groomed, just leave my tummy alone."

No such luck – I growled and attempted to swipe at Lauren as she turned me over, but Lauren, this time, had apparently been expecting this reaction and swiftly moved herself beyond my reach, leaving me sitting there watching William fill my bowls. Thus it was that this hungry cat was left concentrating on just one thing, well two actually – food and water!

I looked around – of course the kitchen door, that led out on to their garden was firmly shut, as was the door to the hall. I decided to be sensible and carried on eating as Lauren busied herself getting breakfast ready.

William studied me intensely, "At least young man, you are not escaping to-day. There is no way out – there is no cat flap in the kitchen door either, although there is one in the shed. We will introduce you to your outside living quarters properly later in the day, because there is no way I am going to risk showing you on my own – we both realise that you are a very wily cat."

I heard a noise in the hall and watched as William duly left and returned carrying their Sunday newspapers, which they duly commenced reading as they settled down to their breakfast.

Lauren eventually opened the kitchen door and then went and opened the living room door for me. I strolled into the living room looking for somewhere to rest. I eyed the ample armchair, noticing the thick cover stretched across it – it looked comfortable and inviting.

"Well try it then, you'll soon be moved if it's not allowed," I told myself, leaping up and doing a few body turns, before settling down. Lauren entered the room and just smiled. I had chosen the right armchair. I slept.

I spent a very comfortable day, to be honest, curled up asleep in the armchair, only stirring myself in order to go to the kitchen for some more food and a drink of water, before returning back to my armchair.

It wasn't an exciting day after yesterday, but it was restful. I noticed that William and Lauren had settled down too, reading their newspapers.

"Strange," I thought, I'm already calling it my armchair, but I am most certainly not staying indoors for two weeks; four and a half months was horrendous enough – I only wish they could appreciate what I had been through." I was however, still very tired and slept for the rest of the day. In fact it was only when William picked me up after their dinner that I was aware just how long I had been asleep.

"Come on Matt, we are taking you to see your outside quarters properly this time."

"Great, I'm going outside!" I was overjoyed and highly curious. "This could be interesting."

I was duly carried outside into the garden, in a very firm grip by William, followed by Lauren. On reaching the shed which was not far from the back door that led into the kitchen, Lauren opened the padlock on the shed door and pushed the catch to open the door and followed William and me inside.

"Come on, you can put me down now," I wanted to shout, but no, William was taking no chances.

"Matt this is one of your beds," Lauren informed me as she pointed to a large lined terracotta coloured basket.

"One of my beds, how many have I got then?" I thought.

"And this is your own personal kennel," Lauren continued, pointing to a large polystyrene box opposite.

"We've lined it with fresh newspaper and a tea towel," Lauren continued. "You will be very snug and warm in there."

"Kennel! I'm not a dog," although I felt like barking as one – that would surprise them! "No doubt about it, sooner, rather than later I am going to have to talk to them or I will be fed a bone next!" Yes, I know that is ridiculous, but it is how I felt.

I then noticed the small square cut entrance to the kennel and despite myself, wondered what it would be like inside. The next moment I found myself being gently pushed through the entrance and into the kennel. I was surprised to find it warm and comfortable, no draughts either – I also felt safe. I wondered if they would let me stay the night, so I poked my head out expectantly.

"We had better show him the cat flap Lauren," William's words broke into my thoughts.

"Cat flap, what on earth is a cat flap?"

I was about to find out as William gently extracted me from my 'kennel' and carried me outside as Lauren locked the shed door. The next moment I found my head being pushed against a small plastic window, with a white plastic surround, set into the wooden shed door.

"Now what?" I enquired of myself as the window began to open.

Then I felt William carefully, but firmly pushing my body. It felt very undignified. Instinctively, I put out my two front legs before my head, shoulders and body entered the shed, my back legs duly followed. I was back in the shed, without them having to open the actual shed door. Then the flap closed behind me, except I didn't get into one! (Flap! Stay awake there!).

"Huh, so that was a cat flap, now how did I get out again? Easy, try the same technique again," so in a flash I exited, straight into William's waiting arms.

"Well done Matt, you are a very intelligent animal, but we'll pop you in again to make sure you really know how to get in and out," William complimented me.

"Thanks, you just called me intelligent and now you want me to do it again!" I was a little angry now – first a compliment, then an insult.

"Okay then, it's going to be a quick in and out," so saying under my breath, I was as good as my word.

Of course, William's arms were there waiting, yet again to gather me up. There was going to be no escaping to-day.

William then carried me indoors and settled me on my dumpy – another bed of sorts – I looked down to check if there was any food and water – there was, but I could do with some more crunchies, so I hopped off and sat in front of the half empty dish. I figured if I sat there long enough, either William or Lauren would notice. Low and behold they did – well they had to learn too, otherwise how could we all get to know each other.

"Night Matt, enjoy your supper and don't forget to use the litter tray will you," Lauren so saying stroked me gently and tickled me under my chin. I liked that – I felt loved - a tinge of happiness flooded through me – I would sleep well tonight.

Monday 6th October

To-day was a very restful one for me, even though I really wanted to be out and about exploring fully my new neighbourhood and having more adventures.

William it seems was off out.

"He's all yours, I'm afraid Lauren, let's hope he doesn't play you up whilst I'm at work – hopefully he might just unwind again, like yesterday. Take care."

I watched as William gave Lauren a loving kiss then making certain I was shut in the kitchen, before he entered the hall, I heard the front door open and close behind him.

I was to learn from Lauren – she chatted to me after William had left – that he worked in an office as a Taxation Manager for a local firm of Chartered Accountants – he was very experienced and proud of what he did.

I spent most of the day sleeping undisturbed, on what I now considered to be my armchair, apart from padding into the kitchen for some food and drink when I stirred myself from my armchair. This might be considered bliss to some cats, but I was bored, I wanted excitement, fresh experiences, in fact life!

By the tale end of the afternoon, I decided to wander into the kitchen where Lauren was preparing dinner. I rubbed myself against Lauren's legs and then sat deliberately making squeaking noises at her, until I got her attention. It worked.

"What is it Matt, you are obviously trying to tell me something?"

I walked purposely across to the back door and continued squeaking.

"I know you want to go out Matt and I really do appreciate your frustration, so when William comes home we'll discuss the possibility of you sleeping outside in the shed tonight – will that make you happier?"

I almost jumped for joy; at last something to look forward to – a night outside and I knew how to get out of the shed too! Would they really let me have some independence.

Now I was impatient for William's return and ran through to the front lounge and leapt on to the windowsill.

"Come on William, please don't be late home, I want to go outside." I pressed my now eager little face against the glass. It was however, another half an hour before I saw William turn into the close and approaching the house.

The evening meal seemed to take ages; when were they going to finish their dinner. In fact it was not until 8 p.m. that I was taken out to the shed. I was now really excited as Lauren carried me outside and gently deposited me inside the shed. Thinking it would be best to behave myself, I popped into my little house, dogs lived in kennels, Matt lived in a house! I realised why there were no draughts in my little house, the entrance faced away from the shed door – very thoughtful of them to position my house thus.

It was then I noticed that my food and water were already there, but was annoyed to see the litter tray. If I was going to be left in my house tonight, I expected my freedom to come and go as well.

"William look, Matt has already put himself to bed in his little house – good boy Matt, sleep tight little one, see you in the morning." Lauren stretched her hand inside my little house and stroked my head before slipping out of the shed. I heard the padlock being snapped shut and the catch being put into place as well.

What I heard next chilled my heart.

"We are going to have to block the cat flap Lauren, otherwise he will escape and there's no guarantee he will come back again – we just cannot afford to take the risk."

I listened intently for Lauren's reply.

I know, but what can we block it with?" came her response.

"Simple, I'll get one of those large bags of shingle left over from the landscaping and put it up against the cap flap – it weighs far too much for him to move, so there is no way Matt can push the cat flap open.

"That's brilliant – at least we'll be able to get a good night's sleep without any worries, whilst he's out here." Lauren's relief at the solution was palpable.

I had planned to sneak out as soon as I heard William and Lauren go inside their house, but instead I heard one of them walking away and then returning, followed by an almighty thump against the door of the shed – it must be the bag of shingle. I listened as William and Lauren walked away and waited for the sound of the kitchen door being closed.

The noise of the bag of shingle had initially frightened me, but now I was curious.

I stirred myself from my little house, padded to the cat flap and gave it a push with my paw – nothing – absolutely no movement whatsoever. I then used both front paws for my second attempt, but still the cat flap didn't move. I was puzzled, annoyed and then angry, for I had had no intention of spending the night in the shed whatsoever. I approached the cat flap once again and this time pushed with my head – again nothing moved. I sat down – this was going to require some serious thinking! It was obvious to me now that the cat flap was solidly blocked.

Tuesday 7th October

William and Lauren had had a good night's sleep and awoke in a good humour. The sun was already up as they drew back the curtains. It was going to be one of those glorious autumnal days. First though they had better get Matt in for grooming and breakfast. Lauren followed William down the stairs and through to the kitchen and the back door. The fresh autumnal air filled their senses as the sun warmed them – it was a good to be alive day.

First, William dragged the large bag of shingle away from the cat flap, then unlocked the padlock, turned the catch to the off position and opened the shed door carefully and expectantly.

"Lauren, Matt's not here!" William called out in amazement.

"Don't be silly William, of course he's there, you know there was no way he could have got out. He's probably hiding behind something in order to terrorise us."

Even so, Lauren still rushed out of the kitchen to the shed to help William look for me. They both double checked the kennel, moved the lawn mower, looked behind the step ladder and even searched inside the cupboard at the back of the shed, before finally admitting to each other that I was not there. Both were totally baffled. William finally locked the shed door and they returned to the kitchen.

"There is no way he could have got out," William echoed Lauren's earlier statement.

"The sack of shingle was still firmly up against the cap flap. I even had to move it, before I could open the shed door," a baffled William continued.

"I believe you William, but we have to face facts – as Matt is not in the shed, he has somehow managed to escape – though heaven knows how – we have just got to hope that he comes back again, like he did when he slipped his collar. I know it's becoming a bit of a nightmare, but I have a very strong feeling that Matt is getting a lot of satisfaction out of his Houdini escapades – he's probably somewhere right now chuckling at the thought of us opening the shed door and finding him gone."

"I couldn't agree more, but I must go to work unfortunately and I don't like leaving you to worry about Matt's whereabouts."

"I'll be fine William. I'll continue to look for him after breakfast; besides who knows he might just turn up as before." Lauren was doing her best to reassure William as well as herself, but deep down she was as worried as she had been the first time I disappeared.

I of course, was hidden close by and sat listening to everything they were discussing about my escape. You may consider this mean, but it was the only way I could think of to persuade them to give me my freedom and trust me.

Lauren and William hurriedly prepared and ate their breakfast. They also cleaned my bowls and decided to keep them in the kitchen, so that if I went to the shed for food and found none there, I would hopefully come to the kitchen door and sit outside waiting. Although both William and Lauren were concerned about my whereabouts, they had begun to realise that I was turning out to be quite a character.

A character or not, as the time approached for William to leave for his office, he found he was becoming more and more agitated, he also didn't like the idea of leaving Lauren on her own, whilst I had not returned. He could escape, albeit temporarily, from my second disappearing act, Lauren couldn't.

Lauren needing a distraction too, took the breakfast dishes through to the kitchen for washing up – she could also watch for my return from the window.

"He's back!" came Lauren's joyful cry from the kitchen as she spotted me walking along the top of the garden wall.

William and Lauren both made for the back door and opened it.

"Matt, how did you get out of the shed? Where have you been? Come in at once, please." The concerned questions came tumbling out.

I leapt from the wall, onto to the top of the water butt and onto the lawn and ran into the kitchen.

I had to admit, I was truly pushing my luck.

"I'm not going to tell you how I got out or where I've been, but it's nice to know you have missed me and are concerned – how would you like to be shut in a shed all night with apparently no way of escape," I muttered silently away to myself as I padded across the kitchen and sat waiting patiently by my clean, though empty bowls.

"That cat really takes the biscuit for nerve and cheek, Lauren. Not only has he frightened both of us again, he then has the nerve to reappear as if nothing is wrong, not only that, he's demanding to be fed!" William exploded, with anger, though tinged with relief.

Lauren felt exactly the same, but scolding me would be pointless, besides she just wanted to sweep me up into her arms and hug me – I could tell. She did. I permitted myself a contented purr and nuzzled Lauren's arm. William looked at his watch.

"I've just got time to get his food."

"It's okay William, I'll look after him, at least you can go to work knowing he's home."

"Thanks Lauren, bye love, see you lunchtime."

"Take care and mind how you go," came Lauren's caring reply. Strange, how she always felt it was necessary to say those words, but somehow it was comforting. She turned her attention to me.

"Well, Matt, like it or not, you are going to be combed first, then fed and you best not struggle either young man, or try to scratch me – remember you want your food!"

I took note of Lauren's words and the firmness of her tone and had the good sense to behave myself, for there was I knew, absolutely nothing to be gained by trying to put my paw down, besides, I had been truly naughty.

So I allowed myself to be combed, fed and watered and duly settled down to groom myself – stupid really when I hated the fur balls that occurred from self-grooming – but that's what cats do - though the daily combing helped an awful lot. Finally satisfied with my efforts, I padded into the lounge, found my armchair, climbed aboard and slept the sleep of a wily, but tired cat. I stirred myself briefly on William's return at lunchtime, but settled down again after receiving somewhat surprisingly, welcoming strokes – I duly purred loudly – it seemed to be the appropriate response, in view of my bad behaviour. I was in fact, still waiting for a proper telling off.

"Hey Matt, don't be so cynical, you have a new home, food, two people who obviously love you and you appear to have been forgiven for your escapades – be grateful," I told myself. "Bet they try putting me in the shed again tonight though," I smiled at the thought – because I would escape, AGAIN!"

Evening duly came and with it bedtime. I was scooped up and deposited in the shed along with my litter tray and sufficient food and water for the night.

"I think we had best put two sacks of shingle against the cat flap tonight, Lauren. I still haven't worked out how he escaped last night, but I can't see him overcoming the weight of two sacks."

"Neither can I," I heard Lauren reply as she and William stacked the two sacks against the cat flap after locking the shed with me inside.

I heard the familiar thump after each sack was placed against the cat flap outside.

"So, it's two sacks tonight then," I smiled to myself. "Are you both going to be surprised again in the morning, because I shall not be here!" I was surprised at my confidence, for surely two sacks would make it harder, but if my method worked last night surely it would work again tonight too.

I sat behind the shed door and waited until I heard the sound of the back door to the house being shut and locked, though the shed housing my kennel, basket and food, was a reasonable distance away, I could still hear. I then settled into my basket patiently passing the time until I could be reasonably certain that William and Lauren had retired for the night.

"Right, it's time to escape again," so saying I padded up to the cat flap. First I pushed firmly against the cat flap with my head – it gave as I had suspected from my attempts the previous night, just a little, despite the second sack. I smiled to myself again, in fact I actually grinned!

"You are going to be really, really perplexed tomorrow when you find I'm not here again, in fact I'm surprised you both haven't managed to fathom out how I escaped the first time." If you haven't already gathered I often talk to myself, it is, though there are exceptions, the only time I can have an intelligent conversation!

I sat down firmly in front of the cat flap and stretched out my right leg, turning my paw round, then spread out my toes and extended my claws. I carefully hooked my claws under the rubber edge of the cat flap and gently, but surely pulled the transparent flap inwards and upwards towards myself. As soon as the flap was opened sufficiently, I quickly ducked my head underneath the flap and let go, so that it rested almost on my neck, at the same time I pushed my left leg into the opening, followed immediately by my right leg. I noted with relief and satisfaction that the tiny gap was still there, despite the extra sack of shingle against the door.

Next, using my front legs and head I now eased my highly flexible body through the cat flap sliding downwards and sideways to my right until, as per my first escape, my front paws touched the ground.

I knew by now that although the gap left at the bottom between the sacks and the cat flap was small, it was just sufficient for me, using all the flexibility in my body, to squeeze my way through and out into the cool night air. Once out I let out a cry of "Yes!" and punched the air with my right front leg – I was out!

As I set out for another night of freedom to explore the neighbourhood I couldn't help but giggle at the thought of William and Lauren's faces in the morning when they came to open the shed door.

"I know, I'll come back early, run along the top of the neighbouring wall and hide behind the water butt and watch – it should be fun."

So a very much free and happy Matt the Cat, I went skipping off to find the chums I had met the previous night.

The air was again quite autumnal.

The sky sparkled with stars and the full moon lit my path as I made my way to the forest. I so wanted to meet up with Nutty and the other squirrels, after all what was the point in making two marvellously clever escapes from my shed, if I had no one with whom to share my exploits.

On reaching the forest, I trotted along the path towards the tree where I had first met Nutty; I deftly climbed it, but to my dismay there wasn't anyone about .

I thought of trying to find their burrow, but after some deliberation decided instead just to enjoy the night air and my freedom, I would tell my friends another day. Perhaps, I might meet some other cats on the prowl. But no such luck – strange.

Wednesday 8th October

I crept back along the wall as dawn was beginning to break and settled down behind the water butt. I allowed myself a short nap, knowing full well that the sound of William and Lauren's back door opening when they went to my shed to fetch me indoors for the morning, would arouse me.

Sure enough, at just on 7 a.m. I pricked my ears up as the back door to the kitchen opened – I duly crept out from behind the water butt and quickly slipped behind a nearby bush facing the front of the shed and peered with a bemused smile on my face as I watched William and Lauren approach the shed.

"Wakey, wakey Matt, it's breakfast time," William called out as he and Lauren dragged the first sack of shingle away from the cat flap

"I am wide awake thanks" thought I, hardly being able to contain myself.

"I hope Matt didn't mind too much his night in the shed," Lauren mused as she helped William to drag the second sack away.

I watched with unconcealed delight as I saw William unlock the padlock, turn the catch and open the shed door.

William stepped confidently into the shed to gather me up, whilst Lauren stood guard in case I tried to make a run for freedom. I noticed William wasn't even too concerned when he couldn't see me immediately – he must have been expecting to see me sitting patiently just inside the shed – so he bent down to peer into my kennel expecting to find me there instead.

"Lauren, Matt's not here!"

"He must be, we've just dragged two heavy sacks away from the cat flap, there is no way he could have possibly got out, he's hiding in there somewhere just to frighten us."

"Okay, you stay on guard and I'll look behind everything in here."

I was now having to put a paw to my mouth to stop myself from laughing. I reckoned correctly that William's commonsense told him Lauren was right, as he proceeded to carefully move my kennel, the lawn mower, other gardening equipment and he even opened up the old kitchen cupboard.

"He's not here, honestly Lauren, though I haven't a clue as to how he could have escaped again." William appeared really worried now, as was Lauren.

I felt I had been watching and listening intently enough whilst William was searching the shed and Lauren stood guard – I really couldn't let their agony go on, so I crept out from behind the bush and crept up behind a very agitated Lauren, whereupon I sat, patiently waiting to be noticed.

"What are we going to do William?" Lauren was really concerned.

Finally, my conscience was pricked, so I gently allowed my body to brush against Lauren's bare legs. She of course, jumped and shrieked.

"William, he's here, behind me." Then she turned quickly and swept me up into her arms. I was now her captive as far as she was concerned, but to me, I was finally home and free to live again, for I had escaped and returned of my own free will three times, surely now they would trust me and not attempt to cage me up again.

Breakfast was quickly made and I was groomed and fed too. I sat and listened silently whilst William and Lauren discussed my behaviour and future.

"Look Lauren, he's escaped from our care three times now and returned, don't you think we can scrap the rules and trust him to be let out on his own when he wishes?"

I waited keenly for Lauren's reply.

"I've been thinking along those lines too, although first I want to know how Matt got out of the shed."

"Well I could tell you, though really I just want to watch and see if you are able to work it out for yourselves, but thanks for the vote of trust and especially for the promise of freedom," I smiled inwardly to myself.

Lauren, I noticed was resolutely determined to solve the puzzle of my escapes and marched off into the shed.

"Can you shut me in and put both sacks of shingle up against the cat flap, because I'm going to stay in here until I work out how Matt escaped."

"This should be fun," I thought, "We could be here all day."

William duly dragged the two sacks of shingle to the door of the shed and laid them against the cat flap – he too, hoped Lauren wouldn't be in there all day. He had to go to work.

"Okay, they're in place, but if you haven't worked it out in half an hour, I'm removing them."

"Alright, half an hour it is."

Unbeknown to me as I sat outside and waited, Lauren was bending down inside the shed pretending to be me. She pushed against the cat flap – it gave a little, but certainly not enough for me to have escaped.

"Right Matt," let's apply your logic – if you couldn't push the flap open, could you pull it open, backwards?"

Lauren bent down once more and using her fingernails, she found she could pull the flap towards her – she was excited now – this had to be the way out. Holding the flap up with one paw Matt must have pushed he head underneath and then rested the flap on the back of his neck. So Lauren slid her arm through the flap as though she were me and came up against the sacks, but just before she touched them she had felt a draught of cool air on her bare arm.

I heard her call out to William.

"There is a gap, but it's to the side and I bet it's downwards too."

It was, of course.

"William, I know how he got out – he couldn't push the flap, so he pulled it in and there's a gap to the right side – we seem to have ourselves a very, very clever cat."

I observed William's delight that the mystery had been solved and was impressed with Lauren's brainwork.

"I know intelligence isn't an animal's prerogative, but I wished you had taken longer to figure my escape method," I sighed to myself.

Of course I knew things would change now that they knew how I had escaped, but in what way? Would they still keep to their earlier remarks to give me my freedom?

In the meantime, I was fed, William and Lauren had their breakfast and at 8.30 a.m. William left for work as usual.

I decided to nonchalantly stroll into the living room and climbed onto my armchair for the morning, getting my "beauty sleep" – well that's what I have heard an adult say. After all the excitement, I was asleep within minutes.

The noise of Lauren getting lunch woke me from my slumbers, so after going through my usual stretching routine first, I jumped off my armchair and padded into the kitchen and sat patiently waiting for some reaction from Lauren when she saw me.

"Hello Matt, I take it you have slept well. You really are a naughty, yet crafty and clever cat, but William and I have decided to give you your freedom to come and go as you please. We think you have terrorized us both enough don't you?

Tempted to just give a plaintiff miaow, I decided it was finally time to trust Lauren so I spoke!

"Great, that is kind of you considering what I have put you and William through, but after being locked up for four months, I couldn't take any more imprisonment, so I hope you can understand my behaviour now."

"You speak!" squealed Lauren in amazement, as the plate that was in her hand crashed to the floor.

Then she just stood there studying me intently.

"I bet you also understood every word that William and I have said about you too. You really are the cat's whiskers Matt."

I listened to her laughing at her own joke – it was a terrible one!

"Yes, I do, but you have to promise that you will tell nobody else, but William please, it has to stay our secret."

"But why, Matt, just think you could become really famous – I could contact Dan Stafford or another well known publicist/spokesman for you," she replied laughingly.

"I don't want fame in any form Lauren, I just want to be loved by you and William."

"I was joking Matt, I have read of so many people being destroyed by fame, William and I would never do that to you."

"Thanks, that's a relief," I was purring now. "Do you mind if I surprise William when he comes in for lunch – it will be fun to watch his face."

Lauren smiled – "You're right there! Just don't do it whilst he's holding his cup of tea or a plate."

I, of course, spent the next quarter of an hour in eager anticipation of William's arrival.

"Just got home in time Little Flower, the heavens are about to open," William stated as he entered the kitchen.

"Little Flower, must be his pet name for Lauren, I wonder what she calls him."

"Hello Little Cherub," responded Lauren as she wrapped her arms round William in a big mutual hug.

"Welcome home William," I piped up as I squeezed between them.

William stepped back in a state of shock.

"Matt can talk!"

"So can you," I cheekily replied.

"Yes, but you are not suppose to be able to talk, at least not to us humans. Why are you suddenly revealing this to us?"

"Because, I now trust you and want to stay here with you and Lauren and be loved again, but it has to be our secret."

"Anything else we both need to know, before I agree," William queried.

"None that I can think of; I spoke to Lauren just before you came home." Strange that having revealed myself to both of them and been accepted, I truly felt at home and safe. I was loved.

"Lunch and "Neighbours," Lauren stated endeavouring to get us all back to normality, as she turned on the television.

I was discovering they were "Neighbours" addicts and had followed the 'soap' since its beginning.

With "Neighbours" over, William gave Lauren and me a hug and departed for work.

I spent most of the afternoon chatting with Lauren telling her about how the Robinsons' had abandoned me. I wanted her to fully understand my behaviour and thus me. I noticed she listened intently and gave me a wonderful cuddle after I had finished my story – I nuzzled my head against her shoulder in response.

"Perhaps you would inform William of all this tonight, it will save me having to repeat it again."

"Of course I will Matt. Do you want to go out; I feel I can trust you now to return for your evening meal."

"Yes, please and I will come back, honest."

Lauren opened the back door and I stepped out on my own, but with permission and trust. Now to explore again, but nearer to home.

"Wow, I had called it home again!"

The afternoon air felt fresh against my face and the breeze flicked lightly at my fur coat as I sauntered off to see what other cats lived in the neighbourhood – it would be good to make new feline friends in the area, besides Nutty and the other squirrels. So off I went with the need to escape from the shed gone forever. Freedom is a truly wonderful thing, but so is trust and having owners and friends who love you.

I HAD A LOVING HOME AT LAST!

THE END

UNTIL MY NEXT BOOK!

RESUME

Valerie Jordan, who lives in Norfolk, wrote the first draft of this Diary in 2002, her late husband Aleyn, giving her the time to be able to do this. It was however, a few years later that she began to complete it due to the loss of her husband in 2003. Since then she has written a further two drafts, the final one being in 2011.

Matt the Cat's character is her own creation and he is pleased that his Diary has finally been published and that his escapades can finally be read. It is a heartwarming, informative and entertaining read, for all animal lovers. Matt is telling all his friends to buy it and Valerie hopes you will too!!!

She has also written short stories, one of which has been broadcast by the BBC's Radio Norfolk and another published on one of their web sites, This Norfolk Love.

Before writing this book, Valerie has since 1988 been setting quizzes. She has set quizzes for the local Quiz League and also ran the Great Yarmouth Area Town Quiz for a number of years as well as the annual Furzedown Hotel Quiz Shield Night. Her Fun Quiz nights at local hotels, in particular the Raynscourt Hotel, commenced in 1991 and she turned professional in 1992, these continued for many years including Turkey and Tinsel breaks from 1996 when she presented a Fun Quiz Afternoon at the Raynscourt Hotel up to 2004 when she retired due to the loss of her husband Aleyn in 2003.

In 1990 she had published her first book "Guess the Question!" one of her own ideas, which always managed to tantalize and amuse and in 1992 "Guess the Question!" Volume Two was published followed by a reprint.

In 2006 she decided to publish her book of Matt the Cat! "Terrible Teasers" which she had been collecting and compiling for fourteen years. She has also had published Matt the Cat! Whiz Kids' Quiz Book along with an updated "Guess the Question!" In total she has had published 7,500 quiz books.

Valerie has also represented Great Yarmouth in 1970 on the Radio Quiz Programme "Treble Chance" against such celebrities as the late Ted Moult, Nan Winton and Neil Durden-Smith. She has also appeared on the television quiz programme "Gambit" with her husband Aleyn in 1979.

Anyone wishing to purchase further copies of "The Diary of Matt the Cat!" should not hesitate to contact her via:-
www.mattthecat.co.uk
Email: VJordan2491@aol.com